Everybody's Daughter

Everybody's Daughter

MARSHA QUALEY

Houghton Mifflin Company
Boston   1991

Library of Congress Cataloging-in-Publication Data

Qualey, Marsha.
  Everybody's daughter / Marsha Qualey.
    p. cm.
  Summary: Unable to decide between two attractive boys, seventeen
-year-old Beamer is forced to examine how growing up in a commune
in the north woods of Minnesota has shaped her personality.
  ISBN 0-395-55870-0
  [1. Communal living—Fiction. 2. Minnesota—Fiction.] I. Title.
PZ7.Q17Ev 1991   90-46286
[Fic]—dc20   CIP
                     AC

Printed in the United States of America

AGM 10 9 8 7 6 5 4 3 2 1

For my father, and in memory of my mother

CHAPTER

· 1 ·

Beamer Flynn lay on her bed and scratched a design on the frosted window with her thumbnail. From that bedroom window in the second-story living quarters above her family's bait and tackle shop she could watch the approach and hear the passing of the east-bound highway traffic, first visible two miles away where the road broke over the forested hill, then lost until it roared past the bait shop. This morning, how-ever, the cold weather had entirely frosted over all the windows in her room, blocking her view of the acres of forest and the black stretch of highway that con-nected her home with the world. Beamer had awak-ened early and immediately felt herself closed in a crystal world, a strangely warm and comfortable ice palace.

She had lain in bed for an hour, waiting for the rising, warming sun to peel back the frost from the window. She had listened to the sparse traffic on the highway and imagined its destination and nature: that would be a highway patrol speeding toward doughnuts and coffee at the nearest truck stop; that's a fuel truck hauling heating oil to the scattered country homes; that's a traveling salesman heading happily toward Duluth after a night in a seedy motel.

A car pulled into the shop's parking lot. Beamer's father came out of the store and greeted Daniel, and Beamer listened as the men exclaimed about the cold while clapping their hands and jogging quick steps in the snow. Beamer began scratching out the words "get lost" in the frost; then, pressing her fingertips against the glass, she erased the message with crisscrossed lines of tiny ovals.

Daniel was one of the family's oldest friends, a former member of Woodlands, the now-disbanded commune her parents had helped form eighteen years ago. She knew Daniel would be at the store most of the morning. He had just checked out of an alcohol treatment center — his second rehabilitation in three years — and Beamer's parents welcomed him at all times for all reasons. It was a small thing to do; they loved him.

Beamer dressed and went downstairs. Her father and Daniel were sitting by the wood stove in the store, fondling their coffee cups and speaking in low tones. Daniel had brought a bag of assorted doughnuts, which was warming on top of the stove. Beamer poked around in the bag, found a plain one, and sat next to her father. She dunked the doughnut in his coffee, chewed, and listened to Daniel, who was telling a joke and happily included her in his audience. She waited for the punch line — it was a long joke — then murmured goodbye and went outside.

She pulled the cuff of her sweater down over her fist and polished the open eyes of a huge concrete fish that stood next to the store's entrance. Wally Walleye, Beamer's younger brother, Johnny, had christened him. The garish purples and greens of the monster fish contrasted with the Victorian facade of the building. The store had originally been someone's summer place, a replica of that owner's city home built halfway between a small lake and a once narrow and gravel-covered road. The road had been paved, repaved, and finally labeled a major highway, and the ever-increasing traffic and widening shoulders had chased a succession of owners from the house.

Beamer's parents had bought the building six years ago, using their share of the money earned from the sale of the commune's business, land, and buildings. They spent eighteen months fixing the house and remodeling the lower level into a store — an unnecessarily long time, but time they claimed they needed to make the transition from being commune members to being small-business owners. They adjusted, and Beamer and her brother settled happily into the luxury of private rooms and bath.

When the commune disbanded, many of the members, the Woodies, stayed in the area. Now they used the bait shop for a meeting place, settling in for evenings of happy chats and weepy confessions among the display freezers of prize catches, tanks of minnows and frogs, and racks of T-shirts emblazoned with leaping fish.

They talked about everything during those evening conversations. Beamer had often cringed and withdrawn when they discussed and relived her birth. They passed around that favorite memory as if it were a friendship quilt, each friend adding and changing: Sue — no, LuAnne! — caught the baby; Jeffrey — no, Peter! — took the pictures; Maud — no, Sam! — cooked the birth-night supper. Three details were intact: it had happened nearly seventeen years ago; the moon had been full (that's how Beamer got her name, Merry Moonbeam Flynn), and Daniel, dear Daniel, had been asleep in the kitchen and missed it all.

Daniel stuck his head out the doorway. "Telephone, dear Moonbeam. I believe it's your young Mr. Reynolds. Would you like me to deal with it?"

Beamer went inside, patting Daniel's arm as she passed him. "I can handle Andy. Thanks anyway, Daniel."

It was Andy. "So, how about a movie tonight?" he said without any preliminaries.

"Am I driving, or are you?"

"You'll be glad to know the car is fixed and I'll drive. If the movie doesn't sound good, there's a party at Wendy's at nine, as soon as her mother leaves for work."

"The movie, as long as it's sexy and violent."

"What a tease. I'll be there at seven."

Beamer replaced the phone and turned her back to avoid her father's calculated indifference and Daniel's wide grin. Her night was taken care of, but the day loomed empty and long.

Her mother and Johnny were gone for the day. And with Daniel hanging around, she wouldn't be needed at the store. The bait shop was the largest, newest store of its kind in the area, "the finest fishing and sporting mecca in the North Woods," a Minneapolis sports columnist had written. When the weather was good for fishing, the store was busy and Beamer worked long hours alongside her parents. This year, however, winter had come late and business was slow. The ice was still thin on some of the lakes and rivers, and only the foolish went out. Three weeks ago, with the first freeze, a few eager fishermen had towed and dragged ice-fishing houses out onto Wapata Lake, the lake behind Beamer's house. For two days the store did a good business in carry-out cocoa, fishing gear, and winter bait. Then the temperature rose, and every day Beamer watched the fishing houses sink slowly. They were the beloved summer workshop projects of men who intended to spend long hours out on the ice, catching cold and later catching hell from the women who weren't welcome. Some of the houses sank entirely out of sight, but some were caught midriff by the next freeze, a lasting freeze that locked the useless, dwarfed houses in place for the whole winter.

Beamer decided to go skiing. She went to her room, stripped to socks and underwear, and stood in front of her dresser, deciding how much warmth she would need. She eyed and fingered the silver-and-blue Lycra body suit folded neatly in the bottom drawer. She had bought it last fall and worn it skiing only once. It screams, "Look at my body, look at me!" she decided. She preferred to be unnoticed.

She finally selected long underwear, pulled it on, and put on her jeans and sweater again. Dressed, she stared in the mirror, confronting her hair, a shoulder-length confusion of near-black curls. She carefully wrapped the mass in an oversized bandana and stuffed the lump into a worn, stretched ski cap. The full cap added three inches to her tall, slender frame. She squashed it down, then plumped it back up. Beamer enjoyed being tall, enjoyed being eye-to-eye with most of the boys she knew.

"You like being tall," Andy had once said, "because you think people won't notice how pretty you are."

"I like being tall," she had replied, "because it's easier to reach into the fish freezer."

Once downstairs in the family's private back room, she put on boots, pocketed gloves, and grabbed her poles. She opened the door to the shop and lifted her poles, signaling her intention to her father. He crossed his legs and stared at her for a long moment before nodding, a silent, grudging approval. Beamer left before he could change his mind. Skiing alone was stupid and dangerous, but what could she do? Andy and most of her friends lived twenty miles away in Grand River, and Johnny had given skiing up for hockey. Stupid and dangerous it might be, but it was often her only escape.

"Stoo-pid, stoo-pid," she muttered, skiing to the cadence of the word. She pushed and glided along

6

the trail that circled the lake. At the high clearing on the north shore she rested. There was little human settlement in the area, and from this spot she could see it all — the bait shop, the waferboard factory, the shantytown of sunken fishing houses. Beamer left the lake trail and took a narrower path into the woods. After a mile the path broke into the open at a small lake, Wilton Lake.

Wilton Lake and the surrounding acreage had for years been owned by a reclusive old man, Randolph Dunn. No one had known much about Mr. Dunn, only that he had moved to the area after his World War II discharge and had always kept one or two dogs, usually golden retrievers. The Dunn property abutted the commune's holdings, and the Woodies had at first been delighted to discover their neighbor. An old-timer, they exulted, one who can teach us things. Two representatives visited Mr. Dunn that first spring. He waved his pistol and sicced his dogs on them, and that was that. Thereafter the Woodies kept their distance. One winter, while on a late-night walk with his dogs, Mr. Dunn had fallen through thin lake ice and caught cold; he had died at home two days later. The ground was frozen too hard for burial, so the body was stored in a hospital locker — sixty dollars' rental — until spring. According to Daniel, who always knew the town gossip and news, Mr. Dunn's cabin, land, car, and dogs passed to a wealthy nephew who lived in Chicago. The cabin stood unoccupied and was now a favorite summer spot for trespassing picnickers and hikers.

7

Beamer caught her breath and shielded her eyes. A column of white smoke spiraled gently from the clearing below; someone was using the Dunn cabin. *That's strange,* she thought. *Maybe it's been sold.* She debated checking out the inhabitants, then pushed off in the opposite direction. "Survival rule number nineteen," she said as she skied. "Avoid strange people when you are alone in the woods."

She was sometimes tempted to ski the trails with her eyes closed. She could do it, she knew them that well. She knew their dips, rises, and curves, the exposed roots and low-hanging branches. She knew which trail led to the stand of rare virgin pine and which ended in the bog. The trail she was on now was the shortest route between the old commune and her present home. It angled sharply away from the lake and after a few yards in the trees dropped down a long, steep hill. Beamer tucked her poles and crouched, riding low and fast. At the bottom she rose and leaned into a turn, then kicked and glided into a sprint out of the woods. The trail ended at the back of a long, flat-roofed building, the sole structure in the small clearing. Beamer stepped out of her skis and through the deep snow to a window. She brushed snow off the glass and looked in, knowing well what she would see, seeing much more than was there. This ugly building had been her first home; she had been born here.

Of the twenty-three people who formed the commune, nineteen were left to sell the property to a real estate developer. Most of the Woodies had been college friends in Chicago. The others were added on in the haphazard way that any friendships or connections are formed — a friend of his, a cousin of hers, somebody's old camp counselor, somebody's classmate, somebody's dentist. Somehow, one spring they had all ended up together in northern Minnesota, clearing land, building shelters, sinking wells, digging latrines.

Beamer had never clearly understood why.

"We wanted to make a small, good world in the middle of a rotten one," her father once said.

"But it failed," she pointed out.

"We survived nearly twelve years."

"Then failed."

"Most of our friendships survived. You and Johnny were born there. We could have done worse."

Beamer's parents had met as university sophomores. They were waiting in the checkout line at a food co-op, and Beamer's mother said she admired the tie-dyed pattern of Beamer's father's shirt. "That's all it took," Beamer's mother often recalled happily. "Your father is a fool for flattery."

Their circle of friends expanded, and they spent long nights and countless hours discussing the world they lived in — how they could change it, improve it, escape it. Then Beamer's grandfather died, leaving her mother a large inheritance. Others pooled their tuition money, sold cars, and withdrew savings. Daniel found the property, agreements were signed, parents were told, and the new life began.

Beamer's birth occurred during the group's second winter at Woodlands. Because resources and room were scarce, the group's babies were planned by a central committee. Beamer's parents were the first couple allowed to get pregnant. Her mother labored for four hours in a corner of the common room, with Beamer's father holding and coaching her. Friends roamed in and out. Two midwives attended: Sue, Woodlands' resident nurse, and LuAnne, an Ojibwa from the nearby reservation, a woman wise in the business of childbirth. Moments after Beamer's birth, she had been wrapped in a soft blanket woven for the occasion, and while her parents cradled and wept over her, the other Woodies celebrated with wine and music.

Now Beamer reached deep into an eave and withdrew a key. When the commune had disbanded, Daniel had bought this distant property for himself, intending to renovate it and live here with his family. But his marriage dissolved and his wife and children moved away. The building remained vacant. Daniel lived by himself in town, in a small apartment above his plumbing shop.

Beamer opened the door and stepped inside. Four families had shared this dorm, which was identical to three others on the property. Each building had a living room, four large sleeping rooms, a bathroom, a pump, a wood stove.

"There's no kitchen," Andy had observed immediately the first time she showed him around, last fall.

"We had all the meals together in a central kitchen building. It was closer to the lake."

"But you said this was the only residence building for two years. What did you do? Cook outside over a fire?"

Beamer laughed. "Don't be silly. We weren't primitive nomads."

"Well, excuse my amusing ignorance, Bea, but I have never lived in a commune. Where's the kitchen?"

Beamer put her arms around him and laid her head against his sweater. "We had one, but it was ripped out and converted into a bedroom after the kitchen hall was built."

Andy kissed her on the top of her head, then gently pushed away. He turned and walked slowly around the room. "It's hard to believe everybody lived in this one building."

"Not for long. Two years."

"How?"

"Bunk beds, mostly. Lots of them. And in the warmer months some people used tents. It worked out."

"This was the living room?"

"The commons. Yes."

"Is this where they had all the group sex?"

Beamer sat on a windowsill. "Don't be so predictable."

"I was just kidding."

"Everybody asks. Some people have even asked if I really know who my father is. What most people

11

don't realize is that it takes a lot of discipline to make a commune work. Discipline and commitment. Group sex wouldn't fit in at all."

"You lived here ten years?"

"Lived here, went to school here for five years. I was even born here."

"Where?"

"This room. That corner."

Andy walked to the corner, closed his eyes, and lifted his arms, his hands palms up.

"What are you doing?"

"Absorbing the vibrations."

Beamer laughed. "Feel anything?"

"Just a draft." Andy sat next to her on the windowsill. "Did all those people watch the birth?"

"Yes."

"Your poor mother."

Beamer shrugged. "It was what she wanted. That's how they did things — together. They even took a vote on my name."

Andy smoothed the hair back from Beamer's face. "Hippie worm merchants."

Beamer pulled away. "Don't joke."

"I wasn't making a joke."

"This is hard for me, Andy."

"What is?"

"Coming here with you."

"Why? Afraid I'll rape you in this secluded spot?"

"Afraid you'll laugh, afraid you'll make jokes about it in letters to your old friends."

"I'd never —"

"Andy, I've listened to you laugh and make jokes about the people up here. And I'm the first to admit some of it's pretty strange. But please, just don't make me one of your targets."

"Of course you're not a target," he snapped. "I don't treat people that way. Especially not someone I care for."

Beamer slid off the windowsill, turned, and leaned her shoulders against the wall. She looked at Andy and noticed again, for at least the hundredth time, that he had eyes the color of dark chocolate. Never calm, they saw so much. Her anger drained away. "I'm sorry," she said. "You're right. I get so defensive about it all that sometimes I forget to laugh. Hippie worm merchants is exactly what they are." She smiled. "And, city boy, that explains why I'm so strange."

Andy cupped his hand on her shoulder and lightly massaged it. He was staring at her in a way that made Beamer uncomfortable. She'd seen that same expression once before, when she had visited him in the school art studio and observed him studying an unfinished drawing. "No," he finally said, "that explains why you're so special."

Beamer locked the door and replaced the key. She stared at the dingy building and shook her head. "Tear it down, Daniel," she said. "It's silly to keep it." She knew he came here often — to replace broken glass, to pick up the litter from picnickers, and to think

13

about his family and the years gone by.

This dorm had been distant from the commune's other buildings, and now a strip of tall pines separated it from the townhouses that had gone up on the lakefront. Beamer scooped up a handful of snow, patted it into a ball, and threw it toward a column of smoke rising from a chimney hidden behind those trees. The snowball soared and disappeared.

CHAPTER
· 2 ·

The renegade cop emptied the chambers of his hand-guns and the movie screen was suddenly filled with dead and bloody bodies. Beamer closed her eyes briefly, then opened them and looked at Andy. He was frowning.

"This is awful," she whispered. "Let's go." He nodded, and they rose and left the theater.

A cold wind met them outside and they paused to pull on hats and gloves and knot their scarves. A bank's temperature sign flashed numbers and Beamer stared at the red digits. "Fifteen below," she said. "Now aren't you glad you came to Minnesota?" Andy grinned, then grabbed her padded hand with his own, and they ran the two blocks to his car.

Beamer sat low in the passenger seat, clapped her hands, and chanted, "Go, go, go," while Andy started the car. It took three tries before the balking engine turned over and started.

"What next?" he said. "The party at Wendy's?"

"No, it's probably been raided by now. Let's do something else."

15

"In this town? Everything closes down at nine. Not that there is anything worth doing anyway."

"Complaining again? I warned you months ago that things could get boring."

"Bloody boring."

"Considering you spend most of your free time with me, I guess I should be insulted."

Andy smiled and kissed her. Beamer removed a glove and traced the line of his jaw with her fingertip. "Apology accepted," she said.

"Back to the original question. What do we do?"

"What are our options?"

"The usual — sex or food."

Beamer laughed. "Andy, someday I'm going to call your bluff."

"Your mother was frosting a carrot cake when I picked you up. Do you suppose there's any left?"

"I suppose."

"Well, then, let's go eat carrot cake."

Andy liked to drive fast. The truck shot down the highway, pulled along by its beam of light, which sliced a narrow path through the endless black night.

Beamer had met Andy the previous summer, just before school resumed. One morning, while taking her daily jog around the lake, she had nearly stumbled over him as he lay on his back across the narrow path. She stopped and stared. He rolled his head toward her, opened his eyes, and smiled.

"Hello," he said. "I fell off the rock." He pointed. "That rock. I was standing on it taking a picture of the bald eagle's nest. I stepped back to frame my shot and just fell off."

"Are you okay?"

"Not really. My leg hurts."

"Can you move?"

"I'd rather not. I think it's broken."

"I'll get help."

He tapped her calf. "Your name is Beamer, right?" Beamer nodded. "I'm Andy Reynolds. My family just moved to Grand River."

"How did you know my name?"

"I saw you at the fair last week with your friends. I was compelled by some strange desire, so I asked somebody."

Beamer smiled. "I'm flattered."

"What vanity. How do you know it was admiration that sparked my interest?"

Beamer resisted the impulse to kick his injured leg. "I'll get help now," she said, then turned and ran home.

While Beamer's father and Daniel carried Andy out and delivered him safely to the hospital, she stayed at the store. She supposed she would see him again.

Two days later she was changing the message on the store's roadside sign when he drove up. He got out of the car slowly.

"Would you look at this cast?" he said. "A simple little bone crack and they stick at least fifty pounds of plaster on my leg." He reached back into the car, pulled out a small wrapped box, and handed it to Beamer. "For you."

17

Beamer walked over to him. "For me?"

"That's what I said."

"Why?"

"For saving my life."

"Don't be silly."

"I'm not so sure; I had been lying there a long time. Aren't you going to open it?"

She unwrapped the box. Chocolates.

"Pretty corny, huh?" he said. "But what else does a guy give a girl on their first date?"

Beamer leaned against the car. "First date?"

"This is it."

"You're pretty damn sure of yourself, aren't you?" she said.

Andy shook his head slowly. "Not at all," he said softly. "Look, I'm going to the summer crafts show in Cass Lake. I'm a potter — well, I try — and I wanted to check out the local artists' work. I thought some company would be nice. So?"

She quickly reviewed her options: selling worms on a slow fishing day; taking a walk with her mother; going on a trip to Cass Lake with this strange boy. "Okay," she said, turning toward the store. "I'll clear it with my parents."

"Hey, bring the candy," he called after her. "We can eat it in the car."

The crafts fair was a pleasant diversion, and Andy proved to be comfortable company. They spent several hours browsing among the displays, sampling the foods and chatting with the various artists. When Andy brought Beamer home, two minutes before her

18

promised suppertime deadline, she agreed happily to see him again on the weekend.

The following Saturday evening Andy arrived early for their date. Beamer ran downstairs and discovered him sitting in the circle of Woodies around the wood stove. Jenny was kneeling by his leg, carefully embellishing his cast with her signature.

"Just a minute, Beamo, then you can have him."

"No," said Sue, "it's my turn to sign."

"I haven't done it yet," said Peter.

Daniel wagged a finger at Andy. "Have her back by midnight."

Beamer closed her eyes and quickly pictured a scene of mass murder.

"Since when does Beamo stay out until midnight?" asked Maud.

"Last year, I think," said Daniel.

"Last March," said Mrs. Flynn. "Don't you remember — she was going to the spring dance with, with . . ." She turned to her daughter. "Who was it, dear?"

Beamer didn't answer.

Mrs. Flynn turned to her husband. "Do you remember?"

"I do, but I don't think it's worth mentioning."

"Who?" several voices demanded.

"Andy, let's go," Beamer said firmly. He nodded, rose, and carefully maneuvered his way through the crowd. He was smiling.

Just as they pushed open the store door to the hot August air, Mrs. Flynn tapped her daughter's

19

shoulder. "Do you need money, Beamo?"

"Mom —"

"My treat, Mrs. Flynn," said Andy. "I was raised properly."

Mrs. Flynn wrinkled her brow. "I'm sure, Andy. However, Beamer was raised to contribute her share. Just because you are the boy —"

"Mom, it's fine. Goodnight." Beamer turned to the crowd in the store. "Don't anybody wait up for me," she shouted. The friends laughed and turned back to the stove. Beamer and Andy walked to his car.

"Does this go on often?"

"I'm afraid so. You were very patient."

"Who are they?"

"I'll tell you sometime. It's a long story. They're here most every Saturday night."

Andy rested his crutches against the car while he unlocked the door. "It was kind of fun in a weird way. But I wasn't sure I'd get out alive."

"Next time —" She caught herself. *Please,* she thought, *please let there be a next time.*

"Yes?" he prompted.

"The next time you don't have to come in."

"That sounds safe. Or better yet, why don't you just wait by the road? I'll slow the car down and open the door. You can jump in."

Beamer nodded and smiled. "I'm willing."

He grinned, positioned his crutches to walk around the car, then stopped. "So who was he?"

"Who?"

"The guy who took you to the dance."

"A classmate. Nobody special."

"Good." He kissed her then, the first time. Beamer looked up after the kiss, a sweet, slow one, and saw her mother and Jenny waving in the doorway.

Andy's father had been transferred to Grand River by the large company that owned the paper mill which dominated the town and emptied its treated waste into the river. "He's the vice president in charge of judicious pollution," Andy often joked. Beamer observed with detachment his parents' and sisters' joyful discovery of rural North Woods life — the lakes, the fishing, the skiing, the slow pace. She had seen it often — the newcomer's initial delight, which slowly and surely gave way to boredom and frustration. Soon enough, she wagered to herself, they'll be complaining about the cold, the summer bugs, the high food prices, the long, lonely winters. In two years they'll be begging to go back to Boston.

Andy didn't share his family's enthusiasm. Uprooted from his lifelong home just a few weeks before the start of his senior year, he had developed a hard, angry resistance to the new environment. A philosophy of "I'll do it, but I don't have to like it" guided his involvement in the new life.

Beamer discovered three things that softened his unhappiness: his art, in which he often submerged himself, missing dates and other commitments; his family, especially the two younger sisters, who

21

adored their only brother; and herself.

She was at first enormously flattered that this good-looking, intelligent, funny, transplanted easterner was attracted to her. And when school resumed she quietly relished the attention and hints of envy their relationship generated. She had dated, but never one boy steadily, and she quickly warmed to his nightly phone calls, the weekly dates, and the amusing, affectionate notes he often left in her school locker. A few weeks after they started dating, however, his youngest sister had let it slip that Andy had a girlfriend back home, a college freshman who wrote faithfully. "Her name's Allison," the other sister supplied, before digging into her half of a hot fudge sundae that Beamer had bought them after a chance meeting on the library steps.

Beamer wasn't surprised. It explained in part his great distress at moving. She never raised the subject, told very few of her friends, and only once or twice grilled Kim and Julie, his sisters, for information about the distant Allison.

Andy had once overheard one of these conversations. After the girls had been chased away by his scowl, he had turned to Beamer. He had never mentioned Allison, but he knew Beamer knew about her.

"Don't you mind?" he said.

"Mind what? That we skipped the party to babysit your sisters? Not too much."

"That's not what I mean. About Allison."

Beamer held his hand and traced his fingers with her thumb. He had spent the afternoon working in the school studio, and specks of clay and glaze were rubbed into his hands. She looked at him and smiled.

"No."

Andy frowned. "Why not?"

"She's a thousand miles away. I'm here."

Andy parked the car alongside the store van. "I'm such a good boy," he said. "Here it is, only nine-thirty and I've got you home safely."

"That's odd."

"Nothing odd about it at all. You always want to leave the movie early and go home."

"No, I mean that car. That's Daryl and Sandra's car. The orange Volvo."

"Who are they?"

"Long-lost Woodies. Well, not really lost, none of them is, unfortunately. Even the wayward ones show up from time to time. Even though Daryl and Sandra live just a few miles on the other side of Grand River, they aren't really close to the other Woodies anymore. But they belong just the same."

Beamer and Andy got out of the car and walked around the building to the back door. They stepped into the entry and removed boots and wraps.

"Your family has the strangest friends," said Andy.

"Let's not get started on my parents' friends again."

"I was just —"

"You're free to stay away from them, Andy. So don't complain."

"If I stay away from them, I stay away from you. Do you want that?"

Beamer kicked her boots into the pile by the sofa. She sat, crossed her legs, and warmed her toes in her hands, then looked at Andy.

"Of course not. Then I'd never get out of here."

He frowned. "Is that all I am to you? A ride out of here on Saturday night?"

"Andy." She picked up his hands in her own. "I was joking."

"I'm not so sure."

She kissed the back of his hands. "I was joking," she repeated softly.

Andy moved closer on the sofa, but paused when the background murmur of Woodie voices heightened.

Beamer closed her eyes. "They don't sound like they're having fun tonight. Daryl must have them stirred up about something. He was always good at that."

"What did Daryl do? Write the commune manifesto?"

"He was the administrator. Handled the business and all that. He and Sandra weren't the first to leave the commune, but their going really hurt. Woodlands didn't survive long without him. Everyone was pretty competent at growing things and making peanut butter, but nobody could understand the accounting. It sounds like they're all in the store. With a little luck we can sneak upstairs and have the kitchen to ourselves." She rose and pulled him up from the sofa. She laid a finger on his lips. "You can finish what you were about to do when we get upstairs."

24

Beamer had just pushed open the door at the top of the stairway when her mother appeared at the bottom.

"Hello, Andy, Beamer. I suspected you two would leave that movie early. Didn't I warn you that there were just a few too many dead bodies? Beamo, could I speak with you? Downstairs."

Beamer looked at Andy and shrugged, then ran down the stairs.

Her mother had gone into the back room, where she was sitting motionless in the rocking chair, her hands clasped and resting on her knees. Beamer waited for her to look up from the floor.

"There's some cake left. Your father and Jenny were somehow persuaded to leave a little for the two of you."

"You called me down to talk about cake?"

"No. It would be better if Andy didn't stay too late tonight."

"No big deal. What's up? Something to do with Daryl and Sandra? I saw their car."

Her mother nodded. "Their daughters are sleeping in your room. You'll need to use a sleeping bag for a few days, I'm afraid. Maybe in Johnny's room. They'll be staying here."

"Why?"

Her mother rose and embraced Beamer. "Sandra's in trouble. Someone's been killed, and Sandra's in trouble."

CHAPTER
· 3 ·

On Saturday morning Sandra had told Daryl that she was spending the night with her sister in St. Cloud. She had said goodbye to the children, put a small suitcase in the car, and driven away shortly before noon. Daryl hid behind the draperies and watched her leave, standing motionless and unresponsive to the squalling children until long after the car was out of sight. She hadn't said why she was going.

The Monticello nuclear energy facility was a half-hour's drive from Sandra's sister's home. Until recently, radioactive waste from the plant had been shipped out of state for storage. Now, however, there was a new waste containment tank at the plant. Because the facility was located in farm country near the Mississippi River, the unproven containment system was controversial. For months the plant had been the site of frequent demonstrations.

Sandra drove for three hours to her sister's house without stopping, and that afternoon she and her sister met with another woman. The three left St. Cloud in the late afternoon and arrived at the plant just as the eastern sky began to darken. They parked directly in front of the main gate, got out of the car, removed their supplies from the trunk, and under the watchful eye of the single guard, who was already phoning a report of their presence, began a protest.

They poured blood-red paint over their bodies and on the snow. On the fence they hung a large sign saying NUCLEAR WASTE WASTES LIVES. While Sandra's companions chained themselves to the fence, she returned to the car. Her instructions were simple: connect the two wires that dangled from the steering column and enter a three-digit code on the small console taped under the dash. She did this, then locked the car and joined her sister and her friend. Just as the guard approached, Sandra chained herself to the fence.

The guard was irritated but civil. He had seen many protesters before. He wandered over to the car.

"Now this isn't a good idea," he said. "There are people inside the plant who are almost done working for the day, and they'll want to leave and go home. So why don't we just move this car and get on with business? You don't want to stay out long in this cold, anyway."

Sandra looked into the distance. A quarter-mile away, a freight train was coming into view, a low, dark snake crawling over the snow-covered grassland. She could feel the ground shake slightly as it grew closer. She turned to the guard. "We'll stay as long as we want to stay. There's a bomb in the car. It will go off if you start or tow the car."

The guard peered inside. He tested the door, shaking the handle. "Bombs are a little extreme for you people, aren't they?"

"We are doing what we must do," said Sandra.

"So will we. Ladies, we will get a locksmith and open the car. We will get a bomb expert and defuse the bomb. We will get a hacksaw and cut you loose from the fence. We will get a deputy and put you in jail."

"That will take time."

"And that's all you want — time for the television crews to get here from Minneapolis and put you on the evening news. I suppose you called them from the café down the road?"

The women didn't speak. That was exactly what they had done.

"You protesters are all alike," the guard said as he walked away from the car.

The explosion whipped Sandra and her friends against the fence. Shards and slivers and spikes of glass and metal scraped their faces and ripped at their clothing. When the air was still, Sandra opened her eyes and saw the guard on the ground. He was covered by smoking debris. Sandra saw no movement, no life at all in his body. She went limp in her chains.

The bomb was a small one, and they had never meant it to be detonated. "A deterrent," Sandra had called it. "It will deter anyone from ending our protest until we are ready to go."

As the medics carried Sandra to the ambulance, she covered her face with her hands and wept.

The Woodies responded to this crisis as they had to all others: those who were at the store stayed there, and those who were not came when they heard the news. Two things woke Beamer late the next morning, the sun shining through the curtainless windows of her brother's room and the sound of her mother and Daniel and some others singing in the kitchen. *One of you crazies killed someone,* Beamer thought, *and all you can do is sing.*

She unzipped the sleeping bag, climbed out, and stood for a moment in her T-shirt and underwear, looking at her sleeping brother. "Don't wake up, little brother," she whispered. "Big sis is rather indecent right now." She thought she remembered a Dear Abby column about brothers and sisters sharing bedrooms. Abby had thought it was pretty sick, and asking for trouble. *I should dig that up and show it to Mom,* Beamer thought as she left the room, moving quickly across the hallway to avoid being spotted by any wandering Woodies. She quickly and quietly dressed in her room — Daryl's children were still sleeping — then went into the kitchen.

Beamer nodded and mumbled greetings to everyone, took two of the rolls someone had brought, sipped from the glass of juice her mother handed her, then went downstairs to the store. Peter, Sue, and Jenny were seated by the wood stove. Beamer looked in the back room for her father but only found Maud and Jeffrey waxing their skis. Their ten-year-old daughter, Alissa, was asleep on a pile of coats. Beamer went back into the store.

"Where's my dad?" she asked the others.

Peter rose and refilled everyone's coffee mug from the pot on top of the stove. "He drove Daryl to St. Cloud. They're going to post Sandra's bond as soon as it's set, then bring her home when they can."

Daryl had squandered his profits from the sale of Woodlands on a sauna and hot-tub business. For all his accounting skills, he had never made a success of it. Beamer didn't ask, didn't need to ask, who was providing the money for Sandra's bond. When it came to their friends in need, her parents' pocketbook was open and full. It was the sort of thing they liked to do.

Jenny motioned to Beamer to take an empty seat by the stove. Beamer shook her head and went out-side. A wall of cold air hit her. She pulled her turtle-neck up to her chin, stretched her sweater down over her hands, and tucked her hands under her arms. The bright sun reflecting off the snow was blinding. Beamer closed her eyes and leaned against the giant fish. "My house is crawling with people, Wally. There are people in my room, my kitchen, my store. Probably someone is sleeping in the bathtub. And they all want something: a place to go, someone to listen, bail money, food. I could use a bomb myself."

Her mother appeared at the door, carrying one of Daryl's girls. "Bea, you really should put on a jacket when you go outside."

"Gee, Mom, do I have one? You mean you haven't given them all to some needy beggar?"

"I could use your help now," Mrs. Flynn said, ignoring her daughter's comment.

"With all these people, you need me?"

"With all these people, I especially need you."

Beamer smiled. Her mother seldom exhibited impatience with the people she loved. This was nice. "Tell them to go home."

"That's the problem. They think that's where they are."

During the morning the shop was beset with phone calls, usually from friends who knew of Sandra's connection to the commune and were calling to hear the latest news. By afternoon, however, the newspaper and television reporters had discovered the connection and begun their siege. The bombing was big news, and the commune in Sandra's background gave the story flavor. With the appearance of the first reporter at the store, the Woodies called a quick conference to discuss a unified response. Beamer's mother was chosen as spokesperson for the group, and many reporters — Beamer counted seven at one point — spent a futile afternoon trying to get the others, especially Daryl and Sandra's daughters, to talk. "Keep those girls away from the reporters," said Beamer's mother. "Don't let anyone with a tape recorder or a notepad come near them."

So Beamer and Johnny guarded their charges carefully. After a late-afternoon snack eaten beside a bonfire, the four were resting against a huge snow dune next to the lake when they spotted an unfamiliar woman walking unsteadily through the snow toward them.

"Look at that, Beamo," said Johnny. "All this deep snow and she's got shiny high-heeled boots on." Beamer and the others lay on their stomachs on top of the dune and watched the woman approach.

"I like the down vest," said Beamer. "Fur-trimmed. I hope there aren't any hunters out today." She stood. "What do you want?" she called to the woman.

The woman halted. "Rae Ramone, *St. Paul Pioneer Press.* The children — I really would like to see the children. You have them, don't you?"

"Please go," Beamer shouted. "Get ready," she whispered to Johnny. He told the little girls to stay down and handed them each a candy bar. They settled back into the snow and munched happily. Johnny started making snowballs.

"I won't be a bother," said Rae Ramone. "I won't frighten them. Just for a moment, please."

"Sorry."

"Then you, how about you? You're Merry Moonbeam, aren't you? That's a marvelous name. You must have a lot to say." The woman began walking toward them again. Johnny stood next to Beamer and handed her his stocking cap full of snowballs.

"Please stop," Beamer called.

"This won't take but a minute," said Rae Ramone. "And I promise you —"

The barrage of snowballs began, each one on target. Rae Ramone teetered on her high heels and somehow managed not to fall. When one of Johnny's shots knocked off her beret she started swearing, a string of crude epithets that Beamer seldom heard, even from the men who frequented the bait shop and fish houses.

"Listen to that," Beamer said loudly. "That woman shouldn't be allowed near children. What a mouth!" Rae Ramone swore again, but kept walking toward them. Beamer smoothed the snowball in her hand until it was hard and icy, then she let it fly. It smacked the reporter's chest and knocked her over. A heel snapped off her boot as she fell. Beamer sighed. "A little violence now and then does us all good," she muttered to Johnny. "Let's go back to the house," she said to the girls, and they walked silently and quickly past the fallen Rae Ramone.

Beamer tucked the girls into bed that night and marveled at how quickly they fell asleep. *They have absolutely no idea what's happening,* she thought as she watched them shift and turn until they settled into a deep, still sleep. The girls had been told almost everything, but it seemed to have little impact; they regarded their visit to the bait shop as a lovely adventure.

Beamer brushed back the hair from Kari's face and pulled the nightgown down over her rump. She zipped up the sleeping bag and repositioned Kari in the center of the cot. Then she turned to tuck in Teresa, who was sleeping in Beamer's bed. She sat on the edge of the bed and smoothed her hand over the little girl's head. Beamer leaned against the headboard and closed her eyes.

Teresa had been the last child born at the commune. Beamer had witnessed Teresa's birth, had been nine years old when she sat quietly in a corner of a room while her mother, Daryl, and the midwife tended Sandra. Births were common by then, and Teresa's was no reason for a party. Besides, the Woodies all agreed, it was spring and few people could be spared from work.

Sandra had pounded on her husband to relieve the pain and Beamer had pushed herself deeper into the corner and covered her eyes. Her mother had finally pulled her away from the wall and displayed the baby. Tired and proud, Mrs. Flynn said, "Here's our new girl!"

Beamer looked at the wet, messy newborn. "She's not ours. She doesn't belong to us. She's theirs."

"Beamer!" Her mother's voice was sharp.

Beamer looked at Sandra. Sandra nodded and winked.

Now the little girl shifted and pushed a bare leg free of the covers. Beamer opened her eyes, blinking away the memory. As she straightened the covers, she studied Teresa's face and saw Sandra's. "Oh, you are your mother's daughter," murmured Beamer.

Sandra had been the first outsider to join Woodlands. Only nineteen years old when she arrived, she had already spent three years hitchhiking across the country, surviving by working odd jobs and living in a series of urban communes. She had read about Woodlands in an underground newspaper.

Though they welcomed her warmly, the Woodies were apprehensive and concerned that any newcomer might unsettle the group's unity. Finally, after several sessions of group consultation, she was invited to stay.

Daryl was soon interested, and they were married within a few months. It was the first wedding at the commune, and the Woodies celebrated it with a day-long party which began with the lakefront ceremony. Beamer was the flower girl. As the group of friends waited by the still, clear lake, applauding and cheering, Beamer laid a path of wildflowers before the approaching barefooted couple.

It was Sandra who urged the Woodies to expand their activities beyond the commune. "You can't make a difference in the world by hiding in the woods and talking to yourselves," she chided. "Things *can* be changed. It *will* happen, but only if we work at it. We must put our faith into action."

The Woodies agreed, but how to do it?

"Food co-ops are starting up everywhere," she said, "and they can't get good peanut butter."

The Woodies pounced eagerly on Sandra's suggestion. Yes, they said, we'll import peanuts and make and sell natural, healthful peanut butter. A service to co-ops! Let's put our faith into action!

The business was successful, but for the newly inspired Woodies, it wasn't enough. They rolled on: Build a greenhouse! Grow and sell chemical-free plants to shops and markets! Put our faith into action! Open our nursery school to poor children in the area — playmates for Beamer and the others! Put our faith into action!

Teresa's leg sprang free again. Beamer replaced the cover. "Faith into action," she said, picturing the words that, with the opening of the peanut butter business, had been carved in the mantelpiece over the dining hall fireplace. She kissed her fingertips and laid them on Teresa's brow. "Faith into action," she repeated. "Well, one of them finally took it too far." She rose, turned off the light, and left.

The kitchen was empty. She poured herself a soda, then called Andy. He answered on the first ring.

"I was wondering if I should call," he said, "so I'm glad you did."

"It's been crazy out here."

"You sound tired."

"I am."

"Well, get some sleep, and we'll talk tomorrow."

They said goodnight. Beamer felt cheered and soothed by the thirty-second conversation.

She went downstairs. Her mother was sitting by the stove in the store, knitting and talking with the few remaining Woodies. She looked up and smiled. "All asleep?"

Beamer nodded. "They were pretty beat. I'm going to bed now myself." The Woodies chorused a goodnight. Beamer's mother just smiled slightly, then mouthed a silent "Thank you."

Beamer climbed the stairs. She lay awake for a long time, until she heard the last of the friends leave and her mother go to bed. She pictured her mother calmly knitting, cooking, answering questions throughout the day's chaos, and she wondered how deep the calm truly was. Then she put it all out of her mind and fell asleep.

CHAPTER

·4·

Beamer and her brother usually rode the schoolbus. On winter mornings it wasn't even light when they waited by the highway. For nearly an hour the bus meandered between the scattered hamlets and isolated country homes, collecting children. They stood in groups or alone at the side of the road, some of them already cold and exhausted from walking from their homes to the stop. The winter afternoons were already growing dark when the bus let the last two riders, Beamer and Johnny, out at the store.

Beamer had long ago discovered that if she tried to study or read on the bus she would get sick, so she spent the time chatting with the people around her — who were younger and less interesting each year — dozing, or staring out the window. Twice a day, five days a week, nine months of the year. She knew the route well. Beamer was now the only high school student on the bus. The others had either started driving themselves or had dropped out of school.

Beamer had once begged to drive. "It can't be because you don't trust my driving. You let me drive on some of my dates with Andy."

"That's only fair," said her mother. "There's no reason why he should always have to come out here to pick you up."

"Well, why not to school?"

"Why waste gas when the bus goes anyway?" said her mother. "Besides, winter driving is no joke."

"Forty miles a day?" said her father. "Forty miles of burning fuel and spitting out carbon monoxide just for your personal convenience? I'm surprised, Beamer, that you even ask."

Beamer had begged only once. When decisions were made in her family, they were assumed to be final.

The addition of Daryl's children changed everything.

"You can take the car this week," said her mother on Monday morning. "Teresa and Kari have never taken the bus to school, and that's the last thing they need to cope with now. Can you imagine — Sandra used to drive them every day, and the bus went right past their door?"

"Imagine that," said Beamer.

Her mother handed her the car keys. "They're yours for the next five days. But lose them, dent the car, run out of gas, or pick up any hitchhikers during the week, and you die. By my hands."

Beamer deposited the girls and Johnny at their school, then drove to the high school. It was a new, sprawling, one-story building on the edge of town. She parked, shouldered her backpack, and jogged across the slushy parking lot. When she walked into

39

the airy atrium-commons, she was besieged by friends, acquaintances, strangers, and one or two sworn enemies. She had almost forgotten she was news.

"I don't want to talk about it," she said repeatedly. The first warning bell rang and the crowd thinned. Beamer trotted across the commons, then sprinted down a long hall. Andy and a few friends were leaning against the wall by her locker.

"Good morning," Andy said, kissing her lightly on the lips.

"Oh my God," said Sarah, "I don't believe it. His lips touched hers."

"He must have forgotten his vows," said Tyler.

"Saint Andrew is a mere mortal," said Wendy. "I've always suspected as much."

During the first week of school Andy had said in a senior seminar on personal relationships that he thought waiting for marriage to have sex wasn't such a bad idea. The statement had quickly become school myth, and because of the ensuing teasing Andy had long since regretted his words.

Beamer threw a sharp look at Sarah. She could almost feel Andy's tension, and she knew he was having murderous thoughts about narrow-minded North Woods idiots. The second warning bell rang, and the others left. "I want to hear the whole bomb story at lunch," said Sarah over her shoulder.

"Softball game," said Beamer. "Besides, haven't you read the papers? It's all there." She waved to her friends as they moved away, then turned and reached into her locker. Andy stroked her back as she leaned over.

"You sure sounded beat last night."

"It was a terrible day. Thanks for not calling. The phone never stopped ringing. Even my mother almost lost her cool a few times." They walked quickly toward their classrooms. The halls were nearly deserted, and Beamer paused outside her room to return his kiss. "I'll tell you everything later." They parted just as the final bell rang.

Beamer was a good student. School was easy and too often became boring. The tedium of daily attendance was relieved by seeing friends during the five-minute breaks between classes and, in winter, playing softball during the lunch period.

"Winter softball is not a game for wimps," she had said to Andy after the season's first game. That day she had grazed her cheek by sliding across the icy outfield on her face and belly after successfully fielding a long ball.

"No wimps, only fools," he had replied. "Why don't you at least wear cleats? There must have been over twenty collisions out there today."

"Not allowed. Definitely not allowed. Slipping is half the fun, and sliding is a real skill."

He had touched her cheek gently. "Your skills are a little rusty, aren't they?"

The softball diamond was laid out on a large frozen pond on county property adjacent to the school parking lot. The games were only loosely organized and

41

not an official school activity; the students who played were responsible for maintaining the field.

Every lunch hour, unless the temperature failed to rise above zero, Beamer and twenty others played ball. The games were restricted to upperclassmen. There was no league, and there were no games with other teams until WinterFest, in late February, when the regular players voted for the fifteen best to compete in a season-ending tournament with other teams from the area. Beamer's batting average was high, her fielding was impeccable, and her ability to throw a ball to home plate while skidding across glaring ice was unmatched. She was a shoo-in for the tournament team.

The games were the lunch period social center. A regular crowd of spectators congregated around a bonfire a short distance behind home plate, roasting hot dogs, heating carafes of cocoa, toasting marshmallows, and cheering the antics and heroics on the playing field.

Softball would be an especially welcome diversion today, Beamer thought as she left her fourth-period classroom and headed toward the locker room. The questioning about the bombing had persisted all morning. Mr. Macauley had even suggested postponing a history quiz for a discussion of "this most reprehensible act." "Don't expect me to contribute anything," Beamer had promptly said. They took the quiz.

She quickly changed into her sweatsuit. As she jogged out to the diamond, she glanced down at her gray, formless body. "That's why I like this sport," she said to two other players as she sprinted past them. "With baggy uniforms like this, you can run and no one notices your breasts bouncing."

Andy was eating lunch with friends by the fire. Beamer stopped and stole half of his sandwich, then trotted out to center field, her usual spot.

It was a routine game. During her second time at bat Beamer hit a solid double, brought in two runners, and then, because the fielder bobbled the ball into a nearby snowbank and could not immediately dig it out, came home herself, sliding down the long icy groove from third base just ahead of the ball. She rose, brushed off snow, turned to give a mock bow to the cheering spectators, and saw Rae Ramone.

The reporter waved and smiled. She was standing with a cluster of students by the fire, roasting a hot dog.

"Hey, Laura," Beamer shouted to one of the players on the bench. "Take over for me, okay?" Laura lifted her hand in agreement. Beamer walked over to the bonfire. "How long have you been here?" she asked Rae.

Rae bit into the hot dog. "Not long. This is my second dog. What a marvelous way to spend lunch hour. Much better than staying in a dreary cafeteria. You're a very good athlete."

Beamer didn't reply. She wondered if her friends would help her pelt the woman with snowballs, or maybe hot dogs.

"Can we talk now?" Rae asked.

"No."

"Your friends have been telling me lots about you."

"What friends?" said Beamer, glaring at the students.

"Not me," said Andy. "Except the stuff about the commune's annual Halloween drug and sacrifice ritual."

Rae smiled. "He's nice, Beamer. Look, I'm sorry I was such a pest yesterday. I deserved worse than what you gave me. But I do want to talk with you. Forget about the bombing. I can understand your reluctance to talk about it, and I admire your loyalty to your friends. But I'd love to hear your story — your childhood, the commune, the bait shop."

"I'm really pretty boring."

"That's a fact," said Jessie. Several others agreed loudly.

"Oh, it's not boring at all," said Wendy. "All that group sex in the commune!"

Rae's eyes widened.

Beamer sighed. "Don't listen to her; there was no sex."

Wendy giggled and laid her hand on Andy's shoulder. "I was kidding. Actually, 'no sex' is a fine and famous commune tradition that Beamer upholds today. With help." Andy slipped from her hand.

"Beamer," said Rae, "I'd love to hear anything. I work for the St. Paul paper, but this could go out to papers all over the country — Detroit, Philadelphia, Miami. You are interesting, Beamer. Let me write about you. I promise I will not ask about and will not mention the bombing."

44

"Oh, no!" someone shrieked on the field, moments before everyone heard glass shattering.

"What was that?" Rae asked.

"A long foul ball," said Beamer. "That's the teachers' parking lot next to the pond. It's the lot closest to the lounge door, so they all park there. I just hope that wasn't a windshield. We pool money for repairs, and the pool is almost empty."

Jeff Whitehorse ran up to Beamer. "My hit. Bea, good buddy, do you want to do me a big favor?"

"What?"

"It's Ms. Elliot's car — the right headlight. You wouldn't want to tell her, would you?"

Jenny's car. Beamer nodded. Jeff blew her a kiss and ran toward the school. Most of the other players followed. Damage to a faculty car automatically ended a ball game.

Beamer looked at Rae, then smiled. "You really want to hear about the commune?"

"Yes."

Beamer waved to the others, who were deserting the field and the fire. Andy shook his head slightly. A warning.

"Okay," said Beamer. "But let me introduce you to someone. I'm not doing this alone."

CHAPTER

·5·

Jenny Elliot was a Woodie. When the group had organized the commune, she had been a twenty-three-year-old high school teacher, already divorced from the man who had waited only until the honeymoon was over to start beating her. It was Jenny who suggested that they settle in northern Minnesota. Her family had spent its summers there. "It will be like having a second childhood," she had said. "Only this one will last a lifetime."

"Jenny was the true believer," Mrs. Flynn once remarked to her daughter. "It often seemed that only her strength, or maybe her passion, kept us going. I think she's probably the only one who still wishes we were together."

Jenny taught school with the same passion she had used to motivate the commune. She taught biology, botany, and environmental science, sponsored three extracurricular groups, and had twice been named Grand River High School's Teacher of the Year.

Beamer left Rae Ramone in the gym while she showered and changed. *I may be about to bare my soul to her,* she thought, *but not my body.* She retrieved the reporter and silently led her through the school to Jenny's room. It was Jenny's free period, and Beamer knew she usually stayed in her classroom.

The door was open and Jenny was alone, reading at her desk. Beamer paused a moment to watch her friend. Jenny sensed her presence and looked up. "Hey, Bea, bored with study hall again?" she said. "Come in." She rose and walked to the door. "I know you," she said to Rae. "You were one of the reporters at the store yesterday."

Beamer introduced them. "Actually," she said, "I came to tell you we broke one of your headlights during softball."

"And you brought the press along? That's not news."

"Well, there is something else." Beamer explained everything. "Rae wants my story, but I could use you. For dates and other facts."

Jenny returned to her desk and sipped from a coffee mug, then she turned to Rae. "The first thing you should know is how special Beamer is to all of us. We would all die for her. Or do worse." She gestured toward the vacant desks. "Okay, let's talk."

They talked for nearly an hour. Rae twice tried to direct the conversation toward the bombing, but Jenny and Beamer were resolute and spoke only of the past. When the bell signaled the end of the period, Rae turned off her tape recorder and slapped shut her notebook. She stood and put on her coat. "Thank you both. It's even better than I imagined. Look for the story in this Sunday's paper." She turned to leave, then paused by the door. "You people really believed in something, didn't you?" They didn't respond.

Beamer spent the rest of the week berating herself for talking to Rae. She dreaded reading the article and refused to discuss the interview with anyone. Though the article hung like a dark cloud over her life that week, however, it was better than thinking about Sandra and Daryl and the bombing. The public's interest in the incident had subsided, but Beamer and her family were still preoccupied with it. On Wednesday Sandra appeared in court and was charged with manslaughter. After posting her bond, she returned to the bait shop with Daryl and Mr. Flynn. They stayed long enough to pack and collect the little girls, and then they left for Minneapolis for further consultation with lawyers.

On Saturday morning Mrs. Flynn came to her daughter's bedroom door three times, trying to rouse her out of bed. "Get downstairs and open up the store," she urged angrily the third time. "The new clerk is starting today, and with your father gone I need you. I'm taking Johnny to hockey practice. I'll be back by noon."

Beamer rolled out of bed. She rose, caught sight of herself in the mirror, and groaned. She walked to her dresser, then turned away and picked up the sweater and jeans she had worn the previous day from the floor. "No problem, Mom," she said to the walls. "I'll make sure those coffee-soaked old men get their bait and doughnuts. The family business is safe in my hands." As she bent to pull on her jeans, she spotted Andy's picture propped against a stack of books on her desk. Beamer smiled. "Today I'll peddle those worms if I have to, but tonight I'm out of here."

That afternoon Beamer was explaining to the new clerk for the third time how to clean the bait tanks' aeration system when the phone rang. She patted the puzzled boy on his arm. "It's only hard the first time. We can do it together after we close the store. Why don't you go help my mother with the display, and I'll get the phone." He relaxed and nodded, then joined Mrs. Flynn, who was struggling with a pop-up tent in the store's camping section.

"I'm coming!" Beamer shouted to the insistent phone. She picked up the receiver hurriedly, and the swaying phone cord knocked over a cup of coffee. Brown liquid spread across a newspaper.

Dammit, thought Beamer. "Lakeside Bait and Tackle," she said cheerlessly into the phone, while unraveling paper towels from a roll and wiping up coffee.

"Good afternoon, Lakeside Bait and Tackle. Can you tell me what's the best bait for catching a cagey sixteen-year-old girl?"

Beamer laughed. "Hello, Andy." She tossed the sodden clump of towels into the trash, then hooked her ankle around the leg of a tall counter stool and pulled it closer. She sat down.

"So, what do I use?" he demanded.

"Chocolates have been known to work."

"You're the expert."

"Have you decided what you want to do tonight? I'm leaning toward food and a movie."

"That's why I'm calling. I've got a problem, Bea."

"Oh, no, Andy, don't tell me you have to babysit. Not tonight. Your parents could find someone else."

"It's not my family. Henry called this morning."

Beamer sighed and chewed on her lip. Henry Altman was Andy's studio arts instructor and his favorite teacher. Andy seldom refused his requests for assistance in the studio.

"It's the kiln."

"Oh, the kiln," Beamer said tonelessly. "What's wrong with it?"

"The thermostat is goofy. It heats up okay but doesn't always hold steady. It needs to be checked every fifteen minutes. We're firing all the freshman class term projects. The firing takes several hours. I'm at the school now."

"So?"

"So I need to stay here and watch the kiln."

"Why you?"

"Bea, I'm surprised you're being so tough about this. One night."

"Andy, it has been a lousy week. And in a few hours the Woodies will begin streaming in with their meatless casseroles for potluck dinner. Then they'll sing songs and play games and hassle me about tomorrow's newspaper article. I don't want to be here. I want to be with you. Can you get someone else to babysit the kiln?"

"No one else can do it. Henry will be here at midnight, but until then, it's me."

"May I come keep you company? I'll bring supper." Beamer pinched the phone cord between her fingers. *I sound so desperate,* she thought. *Well, I feel that way.*

"If you want to."

"How do I get in?"

"I'll prop open the back door, the one that opens onto the courtyard. My car is parked right there."

"I'll be there by seven."

The school door opened noisily. Beamer blinked as the fluorescent light flooded out. She stepped in and, kicking away the slab of wood Andy had used to prop the door, let it close behind her.

Her eyes adjusted to the brightness, and she looked around the large room. There were a dozen long bare tables, their once-smooth blond surfaces mottled and chiseled from years of use. Several empty, paint-splattered easels lined one wall. Beamer wrinkled her nose. The lingering smell of paints, cleaners, and other art materials was strong.

Toxic, she thought. *I wonder if artists tend to die young?*

The pottery studio was behind a partition in the rear of the room, and she walked toward it. "Andy?" she called.

"I'm here."

She found him crouching by the kiln. He rose and dusted his hands on his pants. "Thermostat won't stay steady."

"Too hot or too cold?"

"Fluctuates. Mostly too hot. There are some nice things in the kiln. I'd hate to lose them."

"The freshman projects?"

He nodded. He sat on a table and studied the kiln, and Beamer studied him. He was wearing black jeans and a white turtleneck shirt smudged with clay dust. His blond curls were long and falling over his eyes. He brushed them back with an automatic motion.

"Andy," she said, claiming his attention.

"Yeah?"

"I bet those freshman girls have all fallen in love with you."

He considered this seriously. "I think some of them have." He gave her a sly smile. "I'm just glad to know somebody loves me."

"Well, we take what we can get." She set the bag she had been carrying on a table. "And this is what you get for supper."

"Terrific. I'm starved." He opened the bag and pulled out the contents. Beamer took off her coat and hat and tossed them onto a chair.

"Ah, Bea, fast-food heaven. Double cheeseburgers, fries cooked in animal fat, caffeine-loaded soda." He grinned at Beamer. "I only eat like this when I'm with you."

"Enjoy it. I know I do."

He sat at the table. "Your parents must be heartbroken — their oldest child eating cheeseburgers."

"It gives them something to discuss with their friends. Now let's eat."

While they ate they shared stories, Beamer making Andy laugh with her descriptions of the store's odd moments, Andy venting his frustration with the kiln's dysfunction. Beamer had just begun to describe a young customer's proud display of her string of tiny fish when Andy raised his hands.

"Stop, Bea."

"Why? She was so cute."

"This is just like we're married. It's like we've come home at the end of the day from wherever each of us has been and we're having dinner and we just can't wait to talk to each other." He settled back into his chair. "I kind of like it."

"I liked it until you mentioned the word *married*."

"Don't you ever think about it? About being married?"

"I'm a high school junior, Andy. I never, never think about it."

"I do sometimes. Someday I'd like to be married, like my parents are, or the way your parents seem to make it work."

Beamer stuffed her food wrappings inside the bag. "You'll have to ask Allison, then. I never, never think about it." The joke failed. He crumpled his soda cup and threw it into the trash basket.

"I need to check the kiln," he said. When he had again made the adjustment, he rose and turned.

Beamer had moved to stand behind him, and now they were face to face, eye to eye.

"I didn't mean to upset you," she said. He had a fresh smudge on his cheek. She wiped it away with her thumb.

He relaxed and smiled. "I'm glad you came tonight."

"Me too."

He slid a hand around her neck and pulled her toward him. He kissed her on the forehead, the cheeks, the lips.

Beamer stepped back. "Watch the thermostat, Andy. Too much heat can ruin things."

He grinned. "Okay, Bea. I'll keep it steady."

She squeezed his hand and walked away. She stopped at a display shelf of finished pottery pieces and carefully picked up a large bowl with a smooth, even glaze of dark green. The outer edge was trimmed with delicate blue flowers woven into a chain. "This has got to be yours."

"It is, but why do you think so?"

"It's so much better than the others." She replaced the bowl and pointed to the nearest potter's wheel. "Make me something."

"Bea, it's not that simple. It takes days to make a finished piece."

"I know that. I mean, just make something on the wheel. I want to see how you form it."

"I don't like an audience. It's nothing personal."

"You do it for the freshman girls, don't you?"

"I have."

She raised her eyebrows. "Well?"

"I'm wearing a new shirt; potting is messy."

"Andy, look at yourself. The shirt is filthy. And you can always take it off."

"I never thought I'd hear you say that."

"It will be the only time."

"Ever?"

"Andy."

He grinned and peeled off the shirt.

"An undershirt? I'm disappointed."

"It's cold in Minnesota. I like to be warm. Now sit down somewhere and be quiet." He dusted off the broad surface of the potter's wheel. "I'd rather use the kick wheel, but it's broken. This electric wheel is okay, but just barely."

"Broken wheels and broken kilns. Things are in sad shape here."

He shrugged. "It's the art department, not the football team." He switched on the wheel, which began to spin slowly.

Andy opened a drawer in a nearby cupboard and selected several odd-looking implements. Variations on a stick, Bea decided. He wet a sponge and placed everything on a small table beside the wheel.

"I hope there is some clay," he said. "One of the other students was supposed to have made some." He opened a large plastic container and smiled. "Perfect."

He straddled the potter's seat and with a movement of his foot sped the wheel. He placed the clay. "If it's not centered, I can't get it up. Nothing will form."

He cupped his hands around the spinning clay, and in an instant a mud-gray cylinder rose.

His concentration was absolute and contagious. Beamer felt the tension in her own hands as she watched him work. She was amazed as, with the slightest hand pressure, the slightest thumb movement, he commanded the mass up and down, in and out.

His hair had again fallen over his eyes, and he blew upward to displace it. It fell again, and Beamer nearly reached to stroke it into place, then clasped her hands behind her back. She couldn't disturb him.

He picked up the sponge and held it against the clay's interior wall. The sides pushed out, guided by his hands. Suddenly he stopped and turned from the wheel. The clay kept spinning.

"It's a bowl." He switched off the wheel.

"I can see that. It looks terrific."

"Clunky and thick, actually. I just don't feel like doing more."

"I loved watching you do it. Your hands are amazing."

He wiggled his clay-crusted fingers. "Magic fingers — all the girls love them. Would you like to see what else they can do?"

Beamer smiled. "Not tonight, Andy, I promised my mother I wouldn't stay late. It's snowing, and you know how she worries."

He rose from the wheel. "Just let me clean up and I'll walk you to the car."

Beamer threw away the remains of their dinner, then put on her coat. After washing his hands, Andy crouched by the kiln one more time, made a satisfied noise, then rose. He picked up his shirt and pulled it on.

"Thank you, Andy."

"For what? Putting my clothes back on?"

"For letting me come here. For letting me watch you make the bowl. Now when I know you're here, or when I see one of your finished pieces, I can picture you at the wheel."

He wrapped his arms around her. "Hey, Bea, I like you, too."

"That's not what I was saying."

"Oh yes it was. Why don't you just say it: I like you, Andy."

She touched his forehead with her own and said unintelligibly, "I like you, Andy."

He stepped back. "It's a start. Gets easier the more you do it."

"Mr. Experience."

"That's right." He took her hand. "Bea, I never thought I'd say this, but for some time now I've been glad we moved to Minnesota."

Beamer zipped her jacket. "Yeah."

"That's all you can say? Yeah?"

"I'm glad you moved here, too."

He crossed his arms and frowned.

"Okay, how about 'I'm glad you're here because . . .'" His hair had fallen over his forehead again in a soft mound of curls. "Because," she continued in a gentler voice, "I like you, Andy."

He brightened. "That's better. Nice and clear this time. Can you say more?"

She stepped forward, kissed him, then whispered in his ear, "You need a haircut."

CHAPTER

·6·

When Beamer got home, her father was sitting alone in the kitchen. Beamer hugged him. "Welcome back. It's for good, I hope."

"I hope so."

"When I left there were at least eleven people here," she said. "Where are they?"

"I sent them home. Your mother's in bed."

Beamer sat down. "What's the scoop on Sandra?"

Her father rubbed his eyes and massaged the bridge of his nose. "It's not good. The charge is a serious one, the verdict will be guilty, and she will undoubtedly go to prison."

"Someone was killed. She deserves it."

"She didn't intend to kill anyone, Bea. That is clear, even to the authorities. Otherwise it would have been a murder charge, not manslaughter. She didn't mean to do it."

"But Dad, you have to hate what she did. A bomb, for Pete's sake. And she wasn't even smart enough to find someone who could make a bomb that would work right."

"We all hate it. And I've told her as much."

"Then why are you doing this for her? I know, I know. She and Daryl are old friends."

He lifted her legs onto his lap and massaged her ankles. "Did you knit these socks or did your mother?"

"I did. Answer me."

"Bea, I do indeed hate the fact that she resorted to violence, even unintentionally. She knows how I feel. Friends are never exempt from judgment, but that doesn't mean you stop loving them, and you certainly don't desert them."

"You're so noble."

"Noble, no. Tired, yes." A smile spread across his face. "And looking forward to reading about my daughter, the child of hippies, in tomorrow's paper."

Beamer groaned and swung her feet down. "I had almost forgotten." She said goodnight and got up to go to bed. She stopped in the doorway to say something, but didn't. Her father was deep in thought.

Once she was in bed, she lay awake, the picture of her father troubling her. Just as she drifted off to sleep, she knew why: *He's getting old,* she thought. *They all are. Oh Lord, those people were going to change the world and look at them now. I wonder how it feels to hit middle age and know your dreams just can't come true.*

Beamer rose early the next morning. She dressed and slipped quietly downstairs. She wanted to read the

60

paper and be miserable alone, and she knew that once the Woodies arrived for Sunday morning rolls and coffee, she would have no peace. She started a fire in the stove, then put on her coat and gloves and went outside. The morning sky was dark, with only a thin band of light behind the tall pines on the eastern horizon. Two bright headlights emerged from the dark distance. Beamer waved to the truck's driver as she tossed two bundles of newspapers out the cab window, then sped away. Beamer lugged the papers inside, dropped them by the counter, and clipped the wires. She resisted the urge to rip apart the paper in search of herself and instead made a cup of cocoa. That done, she picked up a paper and sat by the stove.

The story was on page one of the features section, next to a picture of Beamer that Rae had taken in the classroom. Beamer read it through twice, her flush increasing until she moved away from the stove and stood next to the cold window. "Nobody to blame but myself," she said. She thought then of readers in Detroit, Philadelphia, Miami, all spilling their Sunday coffee and dropping breakfast crumbs across the story of her life.

Daniel's car turned into the lot as Beamer heard her mother descending the steps. It was too late to bury the papers in a snowbank.

Daniel was accompanied by Maud and Jeffrey and their daughter, Alissa, who sullenly settled into a corner behind the minnow tank to read. Maud took a newspaper and laid a dollar bill on the cash register.

"Is it there?" she said. Beamer nodded.

Mrs. Flynn set clean mugs by the coffee pot. "We might as well put out the OPEN sign." Beamer nodded and went outside. She dragged the heavy iron easel with the sign down to the roadside. By the time she had returned another car had pulled into the lot. Peter and Sue and their children. Beamer waved and held the door open for them.

"Well?" Sue said.

Beamer shrugged. "Read it yourself." They went inside.

Beamer busied herself with store tasks while the Woodies read the story. She waited on a few customers and played two hands of crazy eights with Alissa, who lost both and retreated unhappily to her corner. Jenny arrived and was greeted by a loud, indignant, and loving chorus.

Maud put her arm around Jenny and read aloud from the paper. "This is rich: 'A beguiling woman with a sometimes frightening intensity . . .'!"

Jenny took the paper. "This is my favorite part. I think she has just captured Moonbeam: 'This girl-woman —' "

Beamer groaned.

" '— whose eyes shift in an instant from childish innocence to jaded mistrust . . .' "

The phone rang. Mrs. Flynn answered, then handed it to Beamer. "It's Andy."

"Andy, it's nine o'clock," Beamer said. "Isn't that a little early for phone calls?"

"Jaded mistrust!" he said. "That's it! That's exactly what I see every time I make a move on you."

Beamer hung up without responding. He deserved worse. The Woodies were all babbling, passing the article around, enjoying themselves and enjoying reading about themselves. They all deserved worse. Beamer felt as sullen as Alissa. She had only herself to blame, she thought for the millionth time. But as she watched them — they had by then been joined by half a dozen others — she understood why she had wanted to tell her story to Rae Ramone: she wanted the world to know what she was up against.

Daniel put down the newspaper he had been reading. "I'm not so sure," he said slowly, "that this is a flattering portrait of us."

Smart boy, thought Beamer.

"Why do you feel that?" asked Jenny.

"Well, this bit on the money." Daniel traced his finger down the newsprint until he found the paragraph. "Here we go:

'The alternative economic philosophy that inspired the foundation of the commune manifested itself in an old-fashioned capitalistic result: money. After several years of steadily increasing sales and profits, the commune's two businesses, Better Butter, Inc. and Nature's Nursery, were sold. Each venture was reported to have netted the commune over $300,000. But the biggest prize was to come. Almost twelve years after the first building was raised and the first well sunk, the group voted to disband. Woodlands was sold to a Chicago real estate developer for nearly half a million dollars. "Faith into Action" was now a credo that each of the ex-commune members could chant all the way to the bank.' "

Daniel slapped the paper. "She makes it sound like we got rich! Like we sold out at the first sign of good money. What she doesn't say clearly is that the money was split into nineteen shares." He refolded the paper neatly. "My plumbing customers will really be slow to pay now." He smiled at Beamer. "But it is a lovely portrait of you, Merry Moonbeam. Maybe you should autograph some of the papers for the customers. I'm sure they'd love it. Charge for the autograph; it's an old-fashioned capitalistic thing to do."

Beamer was saved from responding by her father's appearance. "Didn't I just send all of you home?" he said to nobody in particular. No one answered. He sat on the counter, drank coffee, and read the article. Beamer stood next to him. He made a few noises, and twice looked questioningly at his daughter. Jenny leaned over his shoulder and pointed. "I thought that was especially insightful of our Moonbeam," she said. Mr. Flynn pushed her hand away and continued reading. At last he finished.

"Well," he said, "it's accurate, but it's all wrong."

"What do you mean, Dad?" asked Beamer. "I tried to get everything straight."

"Oh, not anything you said, Bea. That's all fine. The reporter's understanding of it. She just didn't understand anything she was hearing." He shrugged.

64

"But I guess you can't explain faith to people who don't have it."

"She knew that!" Jenny practically shouted. "She said to us, 'You people really believed in something,' and she realized she didn't even know what."

"Oh, Moonbeam of the shifty eyes," said Daniel, "why couldn't you make her see?"

Beamer felt flushed, felt chilled, felt frozen, felt like taking a swing at someone. "Not me," she said, speaking slowly and tersely. "I couldn't. Because I don't believe either. Not any of it. That's the problem. I never asked to have any of you in my life, and I'd just as soon do without you now. Whatever it is you pathetic old hippies had and whatever it is you think you've got now, I don't believe in it." Beamer slammed her cocoa mug down on the counter. The dark liquid splashed onto the stack of unsold newspapers. She walked away, then turned around. "And I hate my damn name!"

She bolted into the back room, where she quickly put on her ski clothes. She was outside strapping on her skis before any of the Woodies had taken a deep breath. She sprinted away, sixteen years of anger and frustration blinding her, so that as she skied along the path toward the woods she was guided by instinct alone.

CHAPTER
· 7 ·

Beamer halted at the north shore clearing. She turned to look homeward and saw several cars leaving the store's parking lot. The Woodies were gone, at least for the day.

"Good riddance!" she shouted. Though the friends would undoubtedly discuss the morning's outburst among themselves, Beamer knew that none of them would ever directly mention it to her. Now that her unhappiness was open, it would fester like an untreated wound.

Beamer resumed skiing, following her customary route into the woods. When she broke into the open at Wilton Lake, she stopped. Smoke was rising from the chimney of the Dunn cabin, and she could see a small car parked under the carport. In the rush and confusion of the past week she had forgotten to mention to anyone that someone was using the cabin. "Avoid strangers," she whispered; then, gambling that the inhabitants weren't hit men or Brink's thieves, she skied toward the cabin. As she approached she saw a young man stacking firewood, ordering the tumbled pile of split logs into a useful pyramid next to the front door. *It looks like he's actually living here,* she thought. *I wonder who he is.* Skiing closer, Beamer allowed herself to be noticed. The stranger smiled, removed a glove, and offered a bandaged hand, keeping it outstretched and bare while he waited for Beamer. They shook hands.

"Hello," said Beamer.

"Hi. Good day for skiing."

Beamer nodded. "I was circling the lake when I noticed life in this cabin. Are you living here?"

"I am. I'm Martin Singer."

"Merry Flynn. We're sort of neighbors. My family has the bait shop on the highway."

"I know. I saw you there this morning; I was buying a paper. Quite a crowd for a Sunday morning."

"Mostly friends. I didn't see you there."

"I saw you. You were playing cards with your sister."

"She's a family friend, not my sister. When did you move in?"

"Ten days ago."

"Is the cabin yours?"

"My father's. He inherited it from an uncle. Maybe you knew him?"

"Not really."

"Crazy, that's the family's story." Martin clapped his hands and blew across his fingers. "This is silly — why don't you come inside? I'm hungry, and I'd love some company."

Beamer considered the offer. Visiting a strange male

in a lonely cabin deep in the woods was probably not smart. *This is my day not to be smart,* she thought. *Besides, he seems harmless.*

A cat bolted out the door as they entered. Beamer moved to catch it. "It's okay if she goes," said Martin. "She comes back." He pulled the door closed behind them and grinned. "My women usually do." He took off his jacket and tossed it on a chair. "Make yourself comfortable while I get things. The tea water is hot, so it will just be a minute."

Beamer slipped out of her ski boots and left them next to a jumbled pile of socks, sneakers, and boots by the door. She looked for a closet or hook for her jacket, found none, so lay it with Martin's on the chair. She began browsing.

She had trespassed here a few times on hiking and skiing trips with friends. They had looked in through the windows and once, caught in a rainstorm, had forced the frail lock and sheltered inside. The lock had slipped easily; others had been in before them.

She recognized the few pieces of big furniture — the scarred table and chairs, the lumpy and worn armchair, the iron-framed bed in the corner. They had all belonged to old Mr. Dunn. Everything else she knew must be Martin's, and the place was cluttered with his belongings. Books were piled on the table, clothes heaped on the bed, papers strewn on the floor, socks hung to dry on the baseboard heater. A disassembled bicycle hung on hooks on a wall, and a small but probably growing pyramid of beer and soda cans stood in a corner.

This is sexist, thought Beamer as she surveyed the clutter, *but I don't get the feeling there are any women living here.* A crystal vase holding two very dead roses stood on the telephone table next to the bed. Beamer tapped the vase, and petals fell off onto a piece of paper. She brushed the petals aside and quickly, inadvertently, read the writing on the paper. "Melissa, Meredith, Kara, Breanna," she read silently. Each name was followed by a phone number. Beamer shook her head. *This guy doesn't waste any time,* she thought. She looked around the room. "A bachelor pad," she whispered. "I'm in a real-life bachelor pad." Still, she had to admit it was warm and comfortable. And quiet — no cackling horde of Woodies. *I like it,* she decided, sitting on the floor in front of the fireplace. She lifted her hands to warm in front of the briskly burning fire.

"Everything's ready," announced Martin as he carried a tray out of the tiny kitchen, which was squeezed into a corner of the big room. He set the tray on the floor. "Sorry about the mess," he said. "I wasn't expecting anyone. Of course, it would probably look like this anyway. I'm not a natural homemaker."

Beamer pointed to the freshly baked bread on the tray he had just set down. "Homemade bread? That's pretty good homemaking."

"Not really. It's frozen dough. You just thaw it and toss it in the oven. I'm not sure how good it is, but it makes the place smell nice. It was really musty in here."

69

Beamer held a hand over her steaming tea mug, then wiped the wet palm on her thigh. "It looks like you've settled in. What are you doing up here? Ice fishing?" *Or are you after some other prey?* she added silently, recalling the list of names.

Martin laughed. "I've never been ice fishing in my life, can you believe it? One of the men helping at your store couldn't."

"Which one?"

"Blond and no beard. He was quite friendly."

"That was Daniel. 'Friendly' hardly says enough."

"Anyway, I am going to be working for a semester at the community radio station in Grand River. It's an internship. I'm a journalism major at Northwestern University."

Beamer couldn't restrain the groan. "Sorry," she said. "I don't mean to be rude, but right now I'm not too fond of reporters."

Martin nodded. "I saw the article in the paper, and I've been following the bombing story all week. I thought the feature today was really nice. But we don't have to talk about it. For once I will stifle my natural inclination to snoop."

"Good." They heard the cat scratching on the door. Martin let her in. After weaving through his legs, she walked to Beamer and took possession of her lap. "Hey, girl," Beamer whispered, smoothing the black fur. "So why did you pick this radio station? Wouldn't you want a bigger place to intern? It's not such a great station. Too much bluegrass music and too much talk."

"I'm hoping I'll get to do more here. Besides, I wanted to live alone in the cabin. That's my real reason — to get out of Chicago for a few months."

"Running away from something?"

"Responsibility," he said, articulating and accenting each syllable.

"The radio station won't be happy to hear that."

"Oh, I'll be very responsible at work. But after hours, well, it's my game."

Beamer again thought of the list of girls. Did they play his game? She sipped her tea and made a face. It was strong and bitter.

"You disapprove?" said Martin.

"Oh, no, it's just the tea. It's a little strong."

He sipped. "You're right. Do you want yours weaker?"

Beamer handed over her mug. Martin returned to the kitchen and continued talking while he boiled more water. Beamer watched him but was soon not listening, ignoring the explanation of journalism school requirements while she memorized his relaxed stance, his casual gestures, the way the worn clothes hung on the muscular figure, the pattern of freckles on the handsome face. *College junior,* she thought. *That would make him about twenty-one.*

Martin stopped talking, and Beamer realized she had been caught staring. She nibbled quickly on a bread crust. "This place looks so different," she said.

He handed her the tea mug and sat down. "You've been here before, then?"

"Sort of. Deserted places are always interesting. We'd come by on picnics and just look around."

"It was a real mess."

She unintentionally raised her eyebrows and smiled.

He laughed. "Messier than this, even. Lots of dirt and litter and broken glass." He held up the bandaged hand. "That's how I did this — inserting new windowpanes."

"Well, I never broke anything." She noticed a pile of photographs next to the hearth, and she picked up several. They were black-and-white shots of scenery. "Yours?" Martin nodded. "They're really nice. This one especially. You've got the snow and shadows just right."

"Thank you. Are you a photographer?"

"No. But a friend of mine is an artist. I've picked up a few things from him. He's always looking at ordinary things and seeing something different."

"He's probably a good artist, then."

Martin's eyes gazed steadily at her. She definitely did not want to start talking about Andy with this guy. "So you shoot pictures," she said. "And if you're in journalism you can probably write. And you bake bread. Is there anything you can't do?"

Martin looked questioningly at her, searching for sarcasm. Beamer flushed; she hadn't meant it the way it sounded. He smiled, removed a boot, and placed it on the hearth, then tugged a second boot free and massaged his foot. Two toes wiggled through a large hole in the gray wool. "Sure," he said, displaying the foot. "I can't darn socks."

They talked for an hour, and for the second time that week Beamer began revealing the secrets of her life. Yet even as she talked she knew this time was different: Martin listened, she felt, without judging. And he didn't take notes.

As the conversation moved along, Beamer relaxed, soothed by the tea, the talk, and the fire. She was somewhere the Woodies had never been; she had escaped them.

Someone knocked at the door. Martin rose and answered it. It was Mr. Flynn. "Could I speak with my daughter? I believe those are her skis."

Beamer glanced at her watch and died twenty times. She had been gone for nearly two hours. Gone by herself, skiing in the deserted, cold, treacherous forest. She quickly imagined what her parents had imagined — her body floating lifelessly in a patch of open, icy water, or some other morbid scene. She rose and went to the door.

"Sorry, Dad," she said, then introduced her father and Martin. She could guess what he was thinking as he studied Martin — *Just what have you been doing to my daughter, young man?*

He shook Martin's hand, then spoke to Beamer. "You had better get home now. We have work to do at the store." He nodded to Martin, then turned away and stepped into his skis.

"I'll just be a minute, Dad," Beamer said. "My things are inside." She retrieved them.

"I'm sorry," said Martin. "I should have thought."

"No problem — he's worried, not mad. I hope."

"That could be worse. I hope they aren't too hard on you."

Beamer skied behind her father, matching the strength and length of his strong, long strides. They didn't speak until later, when they were both working in the store, and then they spoke not of the morning's outburst or of her delinquent excursion but of Martin.

"He's really nice, Dad. You'll get a chance to know him. He's going to be around all winter."

"Andy will love that. Here, scoop." He was cleaning bait tanks, removing the dead and dying fish from the water before the healthy ones started their cannibalistic nibbling.

"Andy will like him as much as I do. Martin has done some really interesting things."

"Beamer, I don't care what he has done. I certainly don't care to hear about it now. I do care that my daughter disappeared for over two hours today and that I found her alone with a young man I have never seen in my life. Your judgment today was faulty, to say the least."

Beamer turned to the minnow tank. She pinched a bellied-up shiner between her thumb and forefinger and flicked it toward the waste bucket. It bounced off the rim and skidded under the soda cooler. "Cut that out," said her father, "and get that minnow."

When she rose from recovering the fish, her father was waiting and watching. He was not happy.

"Beamer, I want you to apologize to our friends."

Beamer deposited the minnow in the bucket and wiped her hands on her apron. "Why?"

"Pathetic old hippies — that's what you called them. We haven't allowed name-calling since you were able to speak. Name-calling, that's why you'll apologize."

A customer came up and asked Mr. Flynn to help him find the ice augers. He was directed to the proper aisle. Beamer resumed her work in the bait tanks. Her father approached quietly from behind and laid a hand on her shoulder.

"Bea, you have been brewing a storm for weeks. That's been obvious to your mother and me. But we didn't know why. She thought maybe it was about Andy. I didn't think so. Daniel thought school, but Jenny doubted that. Maud was concerned about your diet, but few of us wanted to blame eating meat —"

"Dad. No."

"Well, if this is what it's all about, I'm glad it's out. But it is unacceptable to fling it at our friends the way you did. You should apologize."

The customer noisily piled his purchases on the counter. Mr. Flynn walked to the register. Beamer watched him. Her father's efforts at admonishment had left him drained; he wasn't even attempting to talk with the customer. Beamer caught his eye. He smiled wanly.

She nodded. *It won't make things any better,* she thought, *but I'll do it. I'll apologize.*

CHAPTER
·8·

When the Woodies assembled the following Saturday evening, Beamer delayed her departure for a date with Andy in order to speak with them. Andy waited in his car.

Standing by the wood stove, she eyed each of the friends in turn, then said clearly and flatly, "I'm sorry I called you pathetic old hippies. It was the wrong thing to say and the wrong way to say it. I'm sorry."

She ignored the muddle of murmured responses and edged through the circle. Daniel was leaning against the checkout counter. He smiled broadly. "You know, Moonbeam, I never much liked your name, either, but I went along. It was Maud's suggestion."

"What was Maud's suggestion?" asked Maud. She had come up behind Beamer.

"Moonbeam's name."

"Not so. It was Peter's inspiration."

"No, I don't think so," said Peter as he joined them. "I'm certain Sue —"

"Don't tag it on me," said Sue.

"Who, then?" said Maud. The group was silenced by its collective reach for memory.

"Good Lord," muttered Beamer. She zipped her jacket and left.

Martin was approaching the store.

"Hello," he said. "Still open? I need some ski wax."

"Open until eight."

"I was hoping to see you, too. Would you be interested in doing something tonight? A movie?"

Beamer was wearing a hat, scarf, gloves, and down jacket, but the chill ran through. "Thanks," she said after a long pause, "but I have a date." She gestured toward Andy's car.

"Steady date? Steady boyfriend?"

She nodded.

"Figures. Well, have fun." He reached to open the store door.

"Martin," said Beamer.

"Yes?"

"Be careful when you go in there."

"Why?"

She paused. "There are some very strange people in there."

"The Woodies? The people you talked about? I was hoping to meet them."

"You were? Well, have fun then."

She walked toward Andy's car, head lowered against the wind. *Okay,* she thought. *I warned him.*

The Woodies lost no time in evaluating Martin. "He's just marvelous company!" said Maud and Jeffrey.

"Patient and caring," said Jenny. "Funny and smart," said Peter and Sue. "A boy to be proud of," said Daniel, who immediately adopted Martin as his own long-lost son. Always reticent and quiet, Beamer's parents reserved their judgment but simply extended their customary warm welcome.

Martin began work at the station, where the staff and membership had been suffering from budget cuts and battles over program philosophy. Martin refused to take sides and agreed to make coffee. Within one month he had his own half-hour early morning program, "Martin's Place," a personal forum which he used to air his favorite music and to interview people who interested him — a taxidermist, a midwife, a school crossing guard. Beamer's father soon had a regular segment, "Bob's Bait Bets and Fishing Report," on Martin's show.

Beamer now turned the radio on immediately in the morning and lay in bed, putting off the day while she listened to Martin. His voice was lazy and low and provided a gentle rousing on the gray, cold winter mornings.

Martin was often at the bait shop when Beamer returned from school, and the two often went for a quick ski around the lake, stopping at the north shore clearing for a candy bar, a nose wipe, a joke, then sprinting the long last mile to race the quickly settling dusk.

The winter days were lengthening, though, and one afternoon Beamer and Martin took a light picnic when they went skiing. They stopped at the clearing, wiped the snow off a large tree stump, and set out the food.

"Oh, good," said Beamer, "you brought mostly junk food. I never get enough, you know. I was raised on yogurt and soybeans and I absolutely crave sugar and chemicals."

"Have some chips, then," said Martin, handing her a bag.

Beamer lay back against a packed snowdrift and munched. Martin opened a Thermos and poured two cups of cocoa.

"I slept late and missed your show this morning," said Beamer. "How did it go?"

"Today was absolutely the worst day of my life," said Martin.

"Absolutely?"

"Nearly so. I had two guests scheduled — a local cop who goes around to schools talking about sexual abuse and this housewife —"

"I think they're called homemakers now."

"— this homemaker who works as a dancer for stag parties. Neither one showed up."

"Maybe they ran off together."

"Could be. And then this new technician messed things up and all the national news and program feeds were lost and I had to fill in air time. Then there was a budget meeting — do we give air time to 'Popular Politics' or 'Senior Sexuality'?"

"Are you going to eat that Twinkie, or is it for me?"

"For you. I was glad to get away. I need to have friends who don't work at the station. I'm so harassed by the end of the day. I don't know what I'd do if the station staff members were the only people I knew up here."

Beamer laughed. Martin arched his eyebrows in question. What could she say? That she had snooped in his cabin and found a list of women and their phone numbers?

"Martin," she said slowly, "I can't believe for a moment you don't know plenty of people. And I bet most of them are a lot more entertaining than I am."

He smiled. "Maybe. In different ways."

I bet, she thought.

He sipped cocoa. "Andy doesn't mind, does he?"

"Mind what?"

"Our spending time together. Going skiing, talking at the store."

"He's an intelligent person, Martin. He knows people can do things together and just be, well, doing things."

"So he doesn't mind?"

"Actually, I don't know if he knows. I have never felt the need to tell him how I spend all my time." Beamer wiped Twinkie crumbs off her legs and rose. She had never even mentioned Martin to Andy. She began stowing the leftover food in his backpack.

Martin rose. "From what I hear, you two have a pretty decent relationship."

Beamer shrugged. She didn't want to talk about Andy with Martin.

"In my opinion, though, sixteen is a little young to be so steady with someone; you miss out on a lot of fun."

"Your opinion doesn't matter. And I'm almost seventeen."

"Pardon me."

"No steady relationships for you, Martin?"

"I had one. It's ancient history."

"Time for fun now?"

"Time for lots of fun. And Merry, I thrive on fun. Is Andy fun?"

"It's not the first word that comes to mind."

"A couple of girls I've met know him. They say he's called Saint Andrew. You have my sympathy."

"I don't need it, Martin."

"Really? I hear otherwise."

"Martin, those clouds are moving in quickly. Let's head back, okay?"

He slipped on the backpack. "Why do I think you're trying to quell my interest in Andy?"

"Because you're a smart boy. I'll race you back to the store."

"Merry, dear, I can't beat you."

"I know. That's why I like to race against you. Come on, let's go."

At a bend Beamer's ski caught on the icy track and she fell. As Martin sprinted past he shouted, "If I win, I get a kiss." Beamer stared at his back until he disappeared, then pushed up and resumed the race. She couldn't let him win.

Martin was waiting for her at the door of the store, when a huge slab of snow slid off the roof and fell on him. They were laughing as they stepped into the store. Beamer scooped snow out of Martin's collar and threw it back out the door, then turned and saw Andy leaning against the counter. He had been talking with her father.

"Welcome back," said Mr. Flynn. "We were just debating whether to send out a search party."

"But decided it wasn't worth it, right?" said Beamer. "This is a surprise," she said to Andy. "A nice one."

Andy smiled, then offered his hand to Martin. "We haven't met. Andy Reynolds."

"Martin Singer." They shook hands.

Mr. Flynn rose from his stool and walked around the counter. "Whatever he wants, you have my permission, Beamo. Meanwhile, watch the register for me. I have to go put some soup on the burner."

"You're the Martin Singer with the program on KKKJ," said Andy. "I can tell by the voice."

"I am."

"I like your show. Reminds me of radio back home, with the type of music and interviews you do."

"Thanks. Home is Boston, right?"

"Was Boston."

"I spent two summers at Tufts University. I liked the city a lot."

Andy turned to Beamer. "I have to go get some things for my mother at a quilter's at Cass Lake. I thought you might like to come along. I'll buy you supper at Carla's Café."

"No thanks, Andy. Algebra test tomorrow. Sorry."

"Right."

Martin moved to the door. "I've got to go edit some tapes. Nice to meet you, Andy. See you, Merry." He left.

"So that's how you're spending your afternoons," Andy said. "I didn't realize you knew him. He's a real celebrity around Grand River, you know."

"He's living in a cabin near here. The Woodies have more or less adopted him, so he's around a lot. We go skiing sometimes."

"He calls you Merry. Should I be calling you Merry?"

She paused. "No."

"Should I be jealous?"

Suddenly weary of questions, Beamer felt the anger surge. "Jealous? That's a funny question coming from you, Andy." She peeled off her ski gloves, smoothed the fingers, then laid them by the cash register. She cocked her head and looked at him. "If you can have two girlfriends, I can have two boyfriends. Fair's fair."

His face paled in distress.

Mr. Flynn returned. "The soup is safely simmering," he said. "You are free to go to Cass Lake."

"I'm not going, Dad."

"Good, then I won't be eating alone. Your mother and Johnny are eating in town. Andy, can you stay and join us? Onion and lentil soup."

"No, thanks, Mr. Flynn. I really should be going." He turned to Beamer. "Walk me to the car?"

Beamer nodded. "But first let me get out of my ski boots."

Andy helped carry her poles and skis to the back room. While he hung her gear on the family's ski racks, she changed into her soft, lined moccasins, wiggling her toes in the fleece. One of the poles fell from the rack, bouncing noisily against a window and then into a collection of cans bagged for recycling. Andy swore softly and rehung it.

Beamer reached for his hand and squeezed it, enjoying the feel of the skin roughened by clay and glaze. She pulled him down beside her on the sofa. "Andy, relax. It was a bad joke. He's not a boyfriend."

His eyes were fixed on the floor. His jaw was set and hard. She released his hand and sat back. "You don't have to be jealous," she said softly.

Andy turned to face her. He considered her words while studying her face. "Okay," he said slowly, "I won't be jealous." He mustered a smile. "Sure you won't go to Cass Lake with me?"

"I really do have to study. But call me later to say goodnight."

"I always do." They rose and, hand in hand, went out the back door. As they turned the corner of the storefront and walked onto the parking lot, Andy

84

stopped abruptly and pointed. "He's still here. What's the problem?"

Martin was standing by his car, staring down. Andy and Beamer walked to him. Martin looked up. "Hello," he said and pointed to a tire. "It's flat."

"Lucky you noticed before you drove away," said Andy.

"Martin," said Beamer, "have you been standing here all this time just staring at the tire?"

"It hasn't been that long. And yes, I have been."

"Do you have a spare?"

"I guess so."

"Martin!"

"Merry, I have never before had a flat and so I have never before changed a tire. Don't look at me like that."

"I suppose you want me to change it for you."

"Can you?"

"Of course. Give your keys to Andy, and he'll get the jack and spare out." She turned to Andy. "I'll go inside and get a flashlight. It's pretty dark already."

"Well, Bea . . ." Andy's voice trailed away.

Beamer groaned. "You too?"

Andy smiled. "Like the guy said, I've never had a flat so I've never changed a tire. I'll get the flashlight."

"I have a flashlight," said Martin, and he opened the car door and rummaged under the front seat. "We're in luck. Two of them," he said, handing one to Andy. Andy peered into the car around Martin and made a face when he saw the messy interior. Martin grinned. "Car slob," he said. "I admit it. Of course, I'm a house slob too. But then Merry has probably told you that."

Andy stiffened. "I didn't know she knew."

"Martin," said Beamer, "do you want this tire changed?"

Martin was working hard at not looking at Andy and smiling. "Yes, I do, Merry," he said.

"Then be quiet." She took Martin's keys, opened the trunk, and removed the jack and spare. She carried them to the front of the car, where she knelt and felt along the underside. "There is usually a notch or a small dent where the jack is supposed to fit," she said. "Ah, here we go. A little light, please." Martin and Andy knelt on either side of her and aimed the flashlights. Beamer secured the jack and started pumping, and the car slowly rose. She went to work on the tire. "Okay, boys," she said, "now watch and learn."

The three were silent until Beamer let out a sharp, low curse when she accidentally smeared some grease on her ski socks.

Andy sighed loudly. "This is what I've always dreamed of."

"What?" Martin asked. "Crouching on a snowbank in Minnesota in the middle of winter?"

"No: a girlfriend who is skilled in manual labor."

Martin laughed and the light bobbed. "Hold still," Beamer ordered.

"How did you get so good at this, anyway?" Andy said.

"She probably goes out searching for flats to change."

"Drives her car over nails and potholes, just to get a chance."

"No," said Beamer, "it usually happens like this — wimpy men from the city come to the country and need help with the hard things, like changing tires and finding their cars in the dark. Ugh, I hope I can tighten these lug nuts enough."

"Let me do it," said Martin.

"Just hold the light." She finished and rose. "Martin, this is a space-saver spare."

"A small tire. I know that much."

"Right. They're not meant to drive very far or very fast, so get your tire fixed tomorrow. Wilder's station can do it."

"Gotcha."

"Do you want me to pin a note on your jacket?"

Martin turned to Andy. "They don't make them like this in Boston, do they?"

"Cute and feisty?"

"Talented, too."

"That's a fact. Have you ever seen her clean and filet a five-pound walleye? Thirty seconds, tops."

"And I bet she doesn't even smell like fish when you kiss her goodnight."

"Hardly ever. Though sometimes there's a scale or two in that wonderful hair."

Beamer handed the jack to Martin. Andy stood next to her and claimed her dirty hand with a firm grip. Martin stowed the flat and jack in the trunk and tossed the flashlights into the car.

"Thanks a million, Merry. Nice to meet you, Andy." He hustled into his car. As he backed out, he rolled down the window. "Merry, I'll collect my prize later."

Andy dropped Beamer's hand and put his arm around her shoulder. She slipped her hand into his jacket pocket, and they walked to his car.

"Collect what prize?"

"He beat me skiing. He gets a candy bar."

CHAPTER
·9·

"Hey, Beamer," Sarah shouted from the bonfire. "Andy's telling tales about you. Better get over here and defend yourself."

Beamer rose from the pitcher's mound, where she had been kneeling in the snow, knotting together a broken shoelace. The noon softball game was over and the crowd of spectators and players was dispersing. She picked up her mitt and jogged to the small group of friends still gathered by the fire.

"Is that dog for me?" she asked Andy. He nodded, clapped a bun on the charred hot dog, and slid it off the roasting stick. "Thanks," she said. Beamer turned to Sarah. "What tales?"

"Ask him."

Andy zipped his jacket. "Time for class. See you later."

Beamer grabbed his elbow. "What tales?"

He grinned. "Oh, nothing much. Just how you loved humiliating me yesterday simply because I caught you and Martin red-handed."

89

"Red-handed?"

"Covered head to foot with snow, he claimed," said Sarah.

"You'd better confess, Beamo," said Jessie. "You're two-timing Saint Andrew."

Beamer sipped from a cup of cocoa someone had handed her. "Well, wouldn't you? The guy can't even change a tire. And he calls himself a man!"

"I do?"

Everyone laughed. A bell rang and they hurriedly picked up the remains of their lunch. Jessie started to douse the fire with snow.

"Don't bother, Jessie," said Beamer. "I'm staying out a while longer." Jessie nodded, then joined the others who were walking toward school. Andy and Sarah lingered by Beamer.

"I'm leaving after math today," said Andy. "I've got to take my sisters to the dentist, so I won't see you later. Should I call tonight?"

Beamer nodded. "Sure. But early, okay? I've got a paper to finish." Andy tapped her on the shoulder, then trotted toward the school. Beamer turned to Sarah. "Did you finally get excused from study hall?"

"No, I'm not a brain like you, Bea. There's a yearbook deadline coming up, so I'm taking study hall in the journalism lab this week."

"Shouldn't you be going?"

Sarah shrugged. "Five or ten minutes, no one will notice. I didn't know you knew Martin Singer."

"I didn't know you did."

"He spoke to our journalism class last week, and a couple of us have been up to the station. He showed us around. He seems really nice."

"He is."

"Pretty gorgeous, too."

"Observant as always, aren't you?" Beamer sat on the bench behind the fire. She warmed her hands in the pouch of her sweatshirt.

Sarah sat next to her. "So what do you have going with him?"

"Nothing that would interest you. We're good friends, Sarah. He comes by the store pretty often. He talks with Dad, flirts with Mom, and listens to the Woodies."

"And with you?"

"We talk. And ski a lot."

"A lot?"

"Two or three times a week. Why are you so interested?"

"On our visit to the radio station, Megan Sanders stayed behind to look at some of the editing equipment. He asked her out."

"Megan? What did Brett think about that?"

"Oh, she didn't go. She's too tight with Brett."

"That's what I thought."

"I've heard of a few others who have gone out with him, though. Mostly students at the community college. The word is . . ." She eyed Beamer thoughtfully.

"Yes?" prompted Beamer.

"The word is that his cabin is a very warm place to be on a cold winter night."

Beamer laughed. "He said he was having fun."

Sarah tossed a handful of snow into the fire barrel. The heated metal hissed. "Doesn't Andy mind?"

"Why should he? What Martin does isn't his business."

"No, I mean, doesn't he mind your being friends with this great-looking guy who seems to have his eye on every female in town? Doesn't he mind that you're skiing together, all alone, day after day?"

"He asked me if he should be jealous. I said no, so he won't be."

"Trained like a good dog."

"No, he's sensible. He trusts me."

"Trusts you not to pressure him to break up with Allison, at any rate."

"Sarah, I told you about her in confidence."

Sarah looked around. "Do you see anyone else here? I can understand why Andy wouldn't want people to know about her, but I don't see why you care."

"I just do."

"Maybe if everybody knew he had someone stashed away back east, he'd feel he had to choose."

Beamer pulled at the leather lacing of her softball glove, then looked at Sarah. "And that, dimwit, is what I don't want him to do."

"You'd win hands down."

"I'm not so sure."

"What could she possibly have going for her that you don't?"

"They went together for a long time, Sarah. That counts for a lot."

"So Andy doesn't mind about you and this new guy. Strange, I think."

"He does mind, but I can tell he has just decided not to say so. Besides, there's nothing there to mind."

"Don't be so sure. Does Martin have a girlfriend at school?"

"No. There was someone, I guess. He told Jenny they broke up last fall."

"He told her but didn't tell you? That's interesting."

"Why?"

"Obviously, if he thought of you as just a good buddy —"

"A buddy? How insulting. My little brother has buddies. I —"

"— he would talk about his girlfriends with you. But he hasn't, right?"

"Right. But then, I don't often talk about Andy with him."

"You really didn't know he's developing the thickest black book in Grand River?"

Beamer laughed. "Sarah, he's a friend. We ski. The details of his social life have never come up."

Sarah tucked her hands under her legs. "Beamer, to tell you the truth —"

"Please do."

"— I've been worried about you. You're not a lot of fun anymore."

Beamer looked up.

"That's not a criticism, just an observation."

"Sarah, tell me why I should be fun. My family sells fish bait for a living, my house is swarming with

93

middle-aged people having all sorts of problems, and my boyfriend has another girlfriend. Maybe I'm not *having* fun. Maybe I'm just getting by."

Sarah sighed. "When you put it like that, it all does sound horrible."

"Thank you very much."

"Well, change it."

"How?"

"Martin looks like fun. I think you're missing a great opportunity."

"What do you mean?"

"Figure it out. Here's this interesting guy who spends his afternoons with you."

"So?"

"Obviously he's just waiting for some signal."

Beamer prodded a clump of snow with her foot and pried loose a frozen candy wrapper. *Waiting for his prize,* she thought. "I don't think so. Besides, Sarah, there is an age difference to consider. Four years."

Sarah stared at her friend. "Four years? You're worried about four years? Beamo, you were smart enough to vote before the rest of us were out of diapers. Four years is nothing between you and some guy."

Beamer picked up the candy wrapper and smoothed it flat across her thigh.

"You know what you need to do?" said Sarah.

"I'm sure you'll tell me."

"Beamo, you have had a small, closed life. You need to ride away from it on the back of some guy's motorcycle. Black leather, wind in your hair. Get the picture?"

Beamer laughed. "In winter?"

"Break away somehow. Do you figure on Andy helping you do that?"

"Andy is a terrific person. Things are fine."

"Bea, you know how many times you have speculated out loud that he's just dating you to pass the time until he goes to college and back to his girlfriend. Why wait to be dumped? Have a good time while you can. Andy can't complain, and maybe, just maybe, it would make your relationship with him a little bit clearer." Sarah leaned closer to Beamer. "I bet Martin rides a motorcycle," she whispered.

"Sarah, romance with Martin just isn't an option. And that's fine with me. Now, don't you have a deadline or something?"

"You are a puzzle, Merry Moonbeam." Sarah rose. "But that's why we all like you."

"Thanks a lot."

"Are you and Andy coming to Megan's party tomorrow?"

Beamer shook her head. "No. It's his sister's birthday, so Andy is taking her and some of her friends to a movie. Besides, your party is Saturday, and two in a row is more than I can handle."

Sarah shook her head. "His sister's birthday? Are you kidding?"

"He likes his sisters."

"Beamo, it's perfect — let Andy go to the movie and you bring Martin to the party. If you don't want him, at least give someone else a chance. You can always tell Andy you took him so he could meet some nice girls. Not that he's having any trouble doing that on his own."

Beamer scooped up some snow and covered the dying fire. She picked up her softball glove, turned, and walked a few steps toward the school. "Are you coming?" she said. Sarah stepped alongside. "Andy wouldn't fall for that. He knows there are no nice girls in Grand River."

"Which is why he settled for you, right?"

"Exactly."

They stood outside the twin doors that led to the lunchroom and gymnasium. "Oh, Beamer," said Sarah, "be normal. Just once. Grab Martin, come to the party, have some fun. Okay?"

"I might."

"Is that a promise?"

Beamer smiled, lifted her hand to wave goodbye, then opened the gym door. Stepping inside, she let the heavy gray slab slam behind her.

CHAPTER
· 10 ·

"How was the party?" Martin asked as he laid a pair of gloves on the counter and placed a ten-dollar bill beside them. Beamer rang the sale, then handed him his change.

"I didn't go." Some people came in and requested coffee. Beamer directed them to the corner of the store which served as a minicafeteria. "What are you doing today?" she asked Martin when she returned to the counter.

"An interview. It should be pretty interesting. Her name is Alice McCay. She graduated from Radcliffe in 1925, and for her honors project she wrote a series of health-food booklets. 1925! Way ahead of her time."

"Too bad. She probably missed out on making a lot of money."

"Why don't you come along? The store isn't very busy."

"Martin, I get to meet enough weird people here. I don't need to go looking for them."

Martin leaned across the counter, smiled, and said softly, "Please?"

"How far down this road do we go?" Beamer said.

"Seven miles. Not much of a road, is it? That's why I'm glad to have you along, Merry dear, to help push me out of the snowbank when I decide to visit one."

"Oh, great. Forget my wonderful self. It's only my body you want." Beamer slumped. What a dumb thing to say.

Martin laughed. "If it was your body I wanted, and I'm not saying I don't, I would —" The rest was lost in a burst of swearing as the wheel slipped and the car skidded off the road.

It took them twenty minutes to push clear — the car was small, but the ditch and snow were deep — and Alice McCay was waiting anxiously outside her house. "I had just about decided you weren't coming," she said. "People often change their minds. It's so far. Next spring I just might sell the place and buy a condo in town. I've been told I can make a small fortune selling to some young people from the city who want a summer place. Come in, please."

Alice captivated them with her history. Two days after her Radcliffe graduation, she had married a young New York stockbroker. "A suitable match," she explained. "My parents were hoping that after I married I'd settle down and start eating meat again." Two weeks after the wedding her husband quit his job and they moved out to Minnesota, where he became a foreman on a logging crew. "He was suitable," she reminisced happily, "but not in the way my parents hoped for. We had fifty years together. Good ones."

The walls of her house were lined with photographs, old ones that told the history of the north country. While Alice talked, she walked Martin and Beamer around the house, using selected photos to illustrate. She stopped in front of a large one. "That was when we were clearing a road between here and the Bena mill, on Lake Winnibigoshish. We found this marvelous stretch of virgin white pine, but no roads for hauling. Dynamite, that's what we used — dynamite. Blew ourselves a road. Two men died, and I buried them."

"You were part of the crew, then?" Martin asked.

"I cooked. This cabin was the lodge. It held thirty men for a meal." She pointed to another photograph, which showed two long rows of bearded men seated at tables, staring at the camera. "July 4, 1928," Alice said. "During the day, when they were gone, I'd get things done." She smiled proudly. "Like this building. I roofed it myself. Laid the boards, cut the shingles, nailed every one of them in place. And I was five months pregnant. Twenty years later I did it again. The roof, not the baby. I've practically rebuilt this place twice by myself, but the roof was the hardest." She buttoned her sweater. "Come take a look." Martin and Beamer exchanged glances, then Martin clipped the tape recorder to his belt. They went outside.

"I built these steps," said Alice. "I go up often, though usually not in winter." They negotiated the snow-covered steps carefully, then climbed onto the roof. It had a shallow pitch and a wide, level perimeter fenced for safe standing. "How silly of me," said Alice. "Of course you can't see the shingles on the roof with all the snow. Still, the view is wonderful." She swept her arm through the air. "Look at that. After finding this place, I never once thought about going back east. Sometimes I come up here just hoping I can die looking at the view."

The view was spectacular — a panorama of lakes, hills, forest, and endless sky. It was all familiar scenery to Beamer, but even she silently acknowledged that this particular vista was unusually striking. She looked at Martin and Alice. They were staring out at something.

"Music," said Alice. "I can't look at this country from this spot without hearing music. Sometimes just a soft flute, sometimes a whole orchestra."

"You're right," said Martin.

"Flute today, I think," said Alice. "Listen."

While the old lady closed her eyes and listened to her private music, Martin fumbled with his tape recorder. Beamer swallowed a smile and resisted hissing, "Liar." She suspected he heard nothing.

Martin and Beamer refused Alice's supper invitation and said goodbye, promising to return.

"The late winter storms will be coming soon," Alice said as she walked them to the car, "and then you might want to use a snowmobile. The snow just gets so deep on this road. That's how my granddaughter gets in and out. She lives in the village. She wants me to join her, but I won't until I have to. Well, however you do it, come if you can. I'm always here."

Beamer and Martin reached the outskirts of Grand River before speaking.

"Neat lady," said Martin.

"Sure is. You were shameless, though."

"What do you mean?"

"All that business about hearing music on the rooftop."

"There's nothing wrong with letting people hear what they want to hear. It's a useful technique."

"Well, it worked. You charmed her socks off. She's a bit older than your usual victims, but I bet the young ones tumble just as easily."

"Nobody's a victim. Everybody I interview —"

"I wasn't exactly referring to interviews."

"— and everybody I play with is a willing participant."

"Participant in what?"

"Crazy times, quiet times." He faced Beamer and smiled. "The quiet times are best."

"Watch the road, Martin, and quit leering. Hey, we turn that way to go to the bait shop."

"I'd like to drop these tapes off at the station before I take you home. You could come in with me and see for yourself how crazy the place is. Would you mind the delay?"

"If it's not too long."

"When's Andy coming for you?"

"Seven or so. I don't want to be late, Martin. I need to get home to eat and change."

He glanced at her. "You don't need to change; you look fine. But then I suppose you like to look special for the steady sweetheart."

"Don't be obnoxious, Martin. And as a matter of fact, I do like to look nice for Andy. What's wrong with that?" she challenged.

He didn't immediately answer. "Merry, why don't you cancel?"

"What?"

"Call Andy and cancel. Then we don't have to rush anywhere. I'll buy you supper and take you to a party I know about. And you won't have to change."

Beamer spotted the bright lights of the radio station's call sign, four blinking orange letters on the roof of a small cinder-block building. "Andy wouldn't be too happy."

"Forget Andy. What about you?"

"Martin, I want to be with Andy, and I don't want to be late."

"The party should be a good one."

"*We're* going to a party. A birthday party."

He snickered. "Ah, a birthday party." He pulled into the station's parking lot. "Merry, have you ever partied past midnight?"

"No, I haven't. And even if I wanted to, tonight wouldn't be the night. Tomorrow is the Community Fund fundraising breakfast."

"Oh, no, I'd forgotten. I bought a ticket last week from some guy who coaches kids' hockey. Six bucks. Are the Woodies involved?"

"They have been since before the commune closed. Everyone thought it would be a good way to make friends with the townspeople. Mom and I are serving at seven."

Martin parked the car in a handicapped spot next to the station door.

"Not here," said Beamer.

"It's just for a minute. I'm getting you home for that date."

"Not in the handicapped space."

Martin cupped her cheeks in his hands and kissed her. "Your virtue," he said after he pulled back, "is inspiring."

"Now are you satisfied, Martin?"

He looked puzzled.

"You got your prize."

He shook his head slightly. "Andy's got the prize."

They climbed out of the car and walked to the station entrance. Martin paused at the door. "How about a consolation promise?"

"What?" Beamer asked suspiciously.

"Pick me up tomorrow morning and I'll go with you to the breakfast."

"That would be nice."

Martin opened the door. "There might be some good stories there."

The radio station was chaotic. Beamer had never been there before, but Martin had often described the frenzied atmosphere. She backed into a corner, watched, and listened. Martin disappeared into the editing room. Beamer stepped into the reception area and stretched out on the only piece of furniture, an old sofa.

Someone came in. Beamer rolled her head and smiled. It was Elizabeth, the station's program director. Elizabeth sat on the windowsill and lit a cigarette. She exhaled onto the glass, then smeared the fogged spot with her hand. One Saturday night Martin had brought her out to the bait shop. Elizabeth had been guardedly quiet through dinner, but by the time Mr. Flynn was serving tea and baklava she was sharing her life story. Beamer had gone to bed early that night and lain a long time listening in her room, wondering at the strange people her parents attracted and comforted.

Elizabeth put out her cigarette, letting the butt sizzle against the cold, moist glass. "Martin is a saint," she said.

Beamer sat up. "Are there Jewish saints?"

Martin entered, paused to lay a hand on Beamer's shoulder, then went to Elizabeth. "You okay?"

Elizabeth lit another cigarette. "My mother should be half so kind as you. And my husband half so smart."

Martin sat on the sill. "Go talk to Rupert. Apologize. For me. If you don't, he'll ruin all my tapes and botch up everything for everybody for days."

"He's fired."

"You can't fire your own husband. Just apologize."

Elizabeth shrugged. "For you. Why don't you go tell him?"

"Please come too."

"Calm him down first, then I'll grovel and apologize."

Martin nodded, kissed her on the cheek, and left.

Elizabeth shook her head. "So smooth, so manipulative."

"Rupert?"

"No, dear, Martin."

"A minute ago he was a saint."

"He's complex, of course. Attractive men always are. But he always manages things to his view. Do you want to know how he does it?"

Beamer was quite certain she didn't, but she had long ago learned from listening to the Woodies that once a confession, manifesto, or statement was begun, its delivery was unstoppable. "How does he do it?" she said wearily.

"It's that flattering way he listens — it makes the men feel wise and competent and the women feel like they're being seduced." She rose and moved to the door. "Be careful, young lady. What he wants may not be what you want." She left the room.

Beamer checked her watch. "Darn you, Martin," she said. "You promised." She went to look for Martin but found no one, and was deterred from searching further by the sound of angry voices coming from a nearby room. Finding a phone in an empty office, she called Andy. His youngest sister answered the phone, and as she yelled his name it was echoed by a succession of family members. The long wait until he came to the phone was punctuated only by the little girl's intermittent giggles.

"Hello?" Andy said finally.

"It's me. I'm at KKKJ. Could you pick me up here? The sooner the better."

"What are you doing there?" He sounded unhappy.

"Martin dragged me along on an interview and now he's tied up and I can't get home. I know it's early, but can you come?"

"Well, you'll have to wait until I cover my wet and nearly naked body. I was in the shower."

Later, when Andy walked into the station, he looked at Beamer and came to a stop. "Hey, don't bother to dress up or anything. It's only Sarah's birthday party."

"Not only will you have to put up with my clothes, but I don't have any money on me. You'll have to buy supper."

Andy whistled. "You mean I actually get to pay your way for once? Are you sure you want to do this? I might demand a lot in return."

Beamer rolled her eyes. Andy's still wet hair had been frosted lightly by the cold air; she felt tempted to lift her hands and gently crush the crisp cap of blond curls. "Let's go," she said, leading him outside.

CHAPTER
·11·

"This music is awful," Andy shouted in Beamer's ear. Beamer hushed him, then rose from the sofa and made her way across Tyler's crowded living room. Sarah was standing in the doorway, directly under a sprig of mistletoe, accepting birthday kisses from any boy who tried to enter the kitchen.

"Christmas was weeks ago," Beamer said to Sarah. "Where did Tyler get the mistletoe?"

"He saved it just for the party. You can have it next week for yours."

"No birthday party for me."

"Just a nice quiet time with Saint Andrew?"

"Something like that."

Sarah rolled her eyes. "Sounds like fun. Why don't you at least make him get off the sofa and come give me a kiss? My day won't be complete until he does."

Someone turned the volume of the music higher and the crowd whooped as a favorite song began. Beamer shrugged a noncommittal response, eased around Sarah, and went into the kitchen. Tyler and Sarah had been going together since eighth grade, and every year they gave each other a birthday party. Together they had an unusual mix of friends, and Beamer always looked forward to their parties.

She helped herself to two large slices of cake and, balancing the plates on top of cups of soda, cautiously made her way back toward the sofa. Halfway, she stopped to observe Wendy riffling her long fingers through Andy's hair. Andy was not unhappy.

"Here's your cake," Beamer said when she stood in front of him. "That looks like fun," she said to Wendy.

"Confetti," Wendy said. "Somebody popped a bag all over him. There was just a ton of it in his hair."

Andy grinned at Beamer. "It's gone now."

Wendy hopped off the sofa. "That was fun, Saint Andrew. Let's do it again." She was quickly lost among the dancing bodies.

Andy took his cake. He ate a bit and made a face. "Carrot cake? For a birthday?"

"You've always liked carrot cake."

"Well, yeah, but you should have chocolate for a birthday."

Beamer slipped a finger into his shirt collar and lifted out a tiny confetti square. "She missed one."

"I was saving that one for you." He spread the collar open and peered down. "I think there may be more."

Beamer laughed. "By the way, Sarah wants a kiss."

"Looks like she's getting enough. Doesn't Tyler mind?"

"The mistletoe was his idea."

"You can spread diseases that way."

"We've all had chicken pox. Don't be so old."

"I just think Tyler should be jealous."

"What would you know about jealousy?"

They squared off with looks, then he rose, walked resolutely through the dancers, and approached Sarah. The kiss was a long one. As Beamer watched them, she pinched the rim of her plastic cup until it cracked. "Tie game, Andy," she whispered sharply, the words unheard through the loud music. "Now you can stop it."

Andy finally stepped away from Sarah and returned to the sofa. "Let's go," he said.

"Let's dance."

"Let's go."

"Andy, we've been here forty-five minutes and almost that entire time you've sat like a lump on the sofa. Try to have fun."

He brought his face near her own. "Bea, I don't like the music, I don't like the cake, I don't like the keg of beer in the bathroom. You can ride home with Sarah or you can ride home with me. I'm leaving."

She watched him return to Sarah to say goodbye. Sarah made a face at Beamer, then grabbed Andy's arm as he started to head for the closet. He shook free and disappeared through the crowd in a hallway. Sarah pretended to pout.

Beamer stayed on the sofa. Tyler came and signaled an invitation to dance. She shook her head. Finally Andy appeared in the front hall with both their coats.

Beamer swore under her breath. "I should have gone with Martin tonight," she said aloud, though no one could hear. She rose and inched her way around the dancers, then turned to wave to Sarah, who was busy with another kiss.

Beamer took her coat from Andy. "Okay," she said. "You win."

They didn't speak as they walked to the car, or during the first five miles out of town. Beamer watched Andy while she searched her own feelings. The lights from the dash cast an eerie illumination on his face.

"Thanks for leaving," he said at last.

"I wish you hadn't asked, Andy. I wish just once you could loosen up around my friends and accept them. And I don't mean loosening up the way you did with Wendy and Sarah."

"That's not it, Bea. That's not why I was feeling so lousy."

"Why, then?"

"I wanted to be with you."

"Well, you were!"

He pulled the car over onto the shoulder. He closed his eyes and gripped the steering wheel.

"What's wrong?"

He slapped the wheel. "Are you dense? Are you just plain dense? You spent the whole day with Martin. Is it too much to ask that you spend a few hours with me? Just me?"

He shifted and drove back onto the highway. More miles passed in silence. Barely slowing to a safe speed, Andy turned the car into the store driveway. It began a light spin, and they skidded sideways to a spot almost in front of the store door.

"Oops," said Andy, and he grinned sheepishly at Beamer. "A little fast, I guess."

She smiled and leaned over to kiss him. He pulled her close, and his thumb rubbed her neck while they kissed.

"Ow!" he said suddenly, pulling back. "Darn stick shift. May I come in?"

Beamer looked at the dark, empty store, the vacant parking lot. Her parents were at Johnny's hockey tournament. The store was empty — rare for a Saturday night.

"Sure," she said to Andy. "We have it all to ourselves."

She unlocked the back door. Inside, they took off their coats. Andy hooked a finger in her belt loop as they walked up the stairs to the family kitchen. She paused at the top to unlock another door, then pushed it open. The spacious room was dark except for the thin beam from the bold white digits of a clock radio.

Beamer reached for the light switch, but Andy held her arm and pulled her close for a kiss. Then he stepped back.

"Why do you put up with me?" he asked. "I'm moody, I complain, I've got another girlfriend, I've forgotten dates. And it's not as if we have great sex or anything. So why?"

"Picked a funny time to talk, didn't you?"

"This is a great time. We're alone for once; I hardly know what to do. Now tell me, why?"

"You're a nice guy."

"That's it? I'm a nice guy?"

She felt she knew what he wanted to hear — that he was irresistible and she couldn't help loving him. She leaned against the door frame and watched his face, its expression muted by the shadows. "Who knows why anyone likes another person, Andy? I just do. I like being with you. I think you're funny. And your moods aren't that bad — no worse than mine."

"Doesn't take much to make you happy."

"You're like nobody else around here, Andy. I like that a lot. What it all adds up to, I don't know. Do I have to?" She switched on the light. "I'll make some cocoa."

Andy straddled a chair and watched her for several minutes. "I like this kitchen," he said. "I can see why everyone wants to hang out here."

Beamer set two mugs on the table by Andy, then spooned out the cocoa mix. She wondered why he had decided to change the subject, why he was watching her so intently. She avoided looking at him. The kettle of water on the range started making noise. She moved to the stove and watched it.

"It will never boil now," he said.

Beamer didn't answer. Andy went to her and kissed her gently on the neck. *No,* she thought. *No.* It slipped out aloud: "No, don't."

"Don't what? Touch you? Don't kiss you? Don't make love to you?"

She gripped the handle of the kettle. It was warm, and the warmth felt good. She didn't speak.

Andy lifted his hand and with a single finger pressed against her chin turned her face toward him. He stuffed his hands into his jeans pockets. "Bea, we've been going out for six months. And just when I think we should be getting closer, it seems that you have started to draw these lines all around you, and I can't cross them and you won't cross them. And I want to. I want to get closer, I want a sign that I can do that."

"What sort of a sign?"

He didn't answer, except to lift her hand and gently trace her fingers.

"Would having sex be a sign, Andy? Is that what you're saying?"

He dropped her hand. "Bea, you are so, so . . ." He looked around, as if he could find the needed word pinned somewhere on a wall. "So controlled. If we did have sex, yeah, it would be a clear sign that things were moving the right way. God knows you would never say how you feel out loud."

Beamer crossed her arms and turned toward him. "Do you mean, Andy, that if I love you I should prove it? That is the oldest, the oldest —"

"Of course not," he snapped. "Believe me, I'd settle for your saying it."

"Hey, Saint Andrew, whatever happened to the idea of waiting for marriage?"

He stepped away. She had never used the hated nickname before. He brought the mugs from the table. Beamer poured the hot water.

"If people wait, that's fine. That's smart. But I'm ready. Mostly because I want to get close to you and

I don't know how else to do that." He laid his hand on her back and rubbed gently.

Beamer stirred the steaming cocoa. The tapping of the spoon against the ceramic mug was a soft, rhythmic breach of the quietness. His hand moved up and down. It had always felt so good when he had touched her, had held her. But now his hand moving on her back felt like a scalpel making a clean, deep incision. She shivered and stepped aside.

"No, Andy." She shook her head. "No."

He nodded slightly. "Okay, Bea. It's your call." He turned and sat at the table with his cocoa.

She sat and sipped, eyeing him over the mug rim.

He smiled. "Thanks for leaving the party," he said. "Obviously, I needed to talk."

"You've already thanked me. It's no big deal. And I'm glad we talked."

"Your being friends with that guy Martin isn't easy for me. I know I'm not supposed to be jealous of him, and I'm not."

"Good, because there's no reason."

"But I am jealous of the time you spend with him. I'd like some."

"You could have all the time you want, but you're the one who's busy hauling your kid sisters to the dentist or to some movie. Or you're checking the kiln at the studio or staying at home to watch some civil rights documentary with your parents. You can find the time, Andy. I'm always here."

"Okay, how about tomorrow morning? We'll go skiing and take a lunch. Then we'll come back here and I'll spend the afternoon helping at the store and playing cards with your dad and Daniel. If Martin can do it, I can."

Her heart sank. "I can't. Tomorrow is the Community Fund pancake breakfast. The Woodies are involved, and I'm serving."

"A pancake breakfast?"

"It's for charity."

"Okay, I'll come along and help you."

Her heart sank lower. "I promised Martin I'd pick him up. I mean, sure, you can come too."

He stared at her in disbelief. "Two's company, Beamer. I'd be number three."

"Oh, Andy, he's just coming along because he's looking for interviews. And my mother's driving. It's not a date."

He rose and drained his cocoa mug. "Well, maybe I'll see you there. I like pancakes."

He walked to the door. She got up quickly to follow him. He stopped abruptly and turned around and they bumped. They stood still, chest to chest, eye to eye. "I'm going home to write to Allison. I'm going to break up with her, Bea. I'm not sure what I'll tell her, really, except that you are the one who means the most to me. I think she knows that anyway."

He left without a kiss. Beamer set their mugs in the sink and quickly went to bed. Her family would be returning soon, and she didn't want to talk with anyone.

"A long day," she murmured as she crawled under the comforter. She turned off the table lamp and stretched out. Her muscles ached, she thought she could feel a headache starting, and she wanted the day to be over. Mostly she wanted to sleep and not to think of Andy sitting in his room writing to Allison. She squeezed her eyes tight, but she still had a clear picture of him sitting alone, writing.

What would he want now? Now that he'd made his commitment, he'd want something. "Something," she said aloud into her pillow. "Sex, or love. He says he wants time." She reached and pulled back the curtains. The moon was easing over the treetops. "People have always wanted something — my parents' money, their advice, a place at the wood stove." The moon was suddenly eclipsed by a cloud. Beamer let the curtain drop into place, then rolled onto her back and watched the shadows. "Could someone just once not want something?"

She heard the family car drive into the parking lot and around to the garage in back. After a few minutes she heard voices and footsteps on the stairway. Her father and Johnny began foraging for food in the kitchen while her mother came down the hall. She paused at Beamer's door. Beamer quickly closed her eyes and controlled her breathing into a slow, steady pattern as her mother peeked in to check on her. She just didn't want to talk, not tonight, not when she couldn't even think straight.

CHAPTER
·12·

Beamer slept late and had to rush in the morning. As she hurriedly searched in her closet and drawers for something to wear, she berated herself for agreeing to represent the Woodies at the breakfast. The Community Fund was a local program that raised money for a number of nonprofit groups. Years ago, when Woodlands still existed, the Woodies had aligned themselves with the civic program in order to build a relationship with the conservative, suspicious townspeople.

"I'll probably be the only one under forty working there," she grumbled. Then she relaxed, when she remembered Andy's promise to join her. Then she remembered Martin's request to come along and she felt like crawling back into bed. Instead she stared into the mirror, hating what she saw.

"Beamer," her mother called from just outside the bedroom door. Beamer thought about feigning sleep again, then answered.

"I'm up, Mom. I'm just about ready to go." She finished dressing and went into the kitchen.

117

Her mother was sitting alone at the table, still in nightclothes.

"Aren't you going, Mom?"

"I was up half the night with a fever or something, and now I've got a terrible headache. Your dad will have to handle the store, so you're on your own. Sorry, dear. Please make my apologies."

"Martin is coming along; maybe he can be coerced into helping. Even if he doesn't, we'll manage without you."

"How was the party?"

"We left early."

"And how was your night with Andy?"

"He left early."

"Anything wrong?"

Beamer hesitated. Preserving privacy was an instinct developed long ago in commune life; confidences with her mother did not come easily. "He says he's going to break up with Allison."

"The girlfriend back east?"

Beamer nodded.

Her mother lowered her head into her hand and massaged her temples. "That's nice."

"I guess."

Mrs. Flynn looked at her daughter. "He cares for you, Bea. Don't let that scare you."

The wind had risen with the sun and was blowing hard when Beamer arrived at Martin's. She ran from her car to his front door, banged a few times, then tried the knob. It was locked. She knocked again. "Oh, Martin, it's cold," she moaned. "Come on, wake up." Just as she decided to leave without him, the door opened and there was a sleepy Martin, ready to go.

"Sorry," he said, "but here I am."

They ran to her car. The warm air they released when they opened the doors blew up a wall of swirling snow.

"Lousy day," said Martin when they were inside. "That wind is just wicked."

Beamer nodded and twisted around to back the car up. She spotted another car parked behind Martin's under his carport.

"Whose car is that?" she said. "Someone you met at the party?"

Martin adjusted his scarf. "I didn't go to the party. It's Elizabeth's car."

"Why is it here?"

"Because she's here. Now let's get going."

They drove toward town in silence. Beamer absorbed this new information and realized she didn't know what it meant.

"She spent the night with you, Martin?"

"She had a fight with her husband and didn't want to go home."

"That's all?"

"I imagine if you've been married for twenty years it's a pretty big deal. She was upset. You saw her last night. She was mad at the world."

"So she came home with you?"

"Where's your mom? Wasn't she going to come?"

"She's sick. I can't believe you would spend the night with a middle-aged woman. Especially a married one. What a scab."

"Maybe you don't know everything."

"I'm sure I don't."

They didn't speak again until they reached the community center. The longest twenty minutes of her life, Beamer decided. "I will never live in the country again," she said to herself as she followed Martin into the warm building. "You spend too much time not talking to people in cars."

The cafeteria was packed, and Beamer quickly took a place beside Peter and Sue in the serving line. She had been doing this for six years. It was easy and — when she would admit it — fun.

Twenty minutes later she felt arms around her waist, and after handing portly Judge Reitman his plate, she turned to see Martin, who was tying an apron around her middle. He smiled. "Scab," she hissed, but with a smile. He let his hand drift across her back as he walked away.

Three hundred people could eat at one time in the dining room, and this morning the room was filled. After an hour Beamer slipped away to eat. No sooner had she sat at the end of a table than Martin appeared with his own plate of pancakes and sausage. He eased a chair into the spot beside her, nodding to the woman who had moved to give him room. Beamer pointed to the chair across the table. "Sit there, scab."

"I want to talk," he said.

"I want to eat. Can I have some of your coffee?"

"First of all," he said in lowered tones, "I did not sleep with Elizabeth last night, or any other night, for that matter."

"Then from what I hear, she's the first."

"No." He shook his head. "You're the first."

"Playing tomcat is dangerous, Martin."

"She just needed a place to stay, and I'm a friend."

Beamer sipped his coffee. It was tepid, and she made a face. "Hasn't she got other friends? Female ones?"

He ignored her question. "And she's not the sort I'd be likely to get involved with."

Beamer faced Martin. "I've been told I should get involved with you. Am I the right sort?" She wanted the words back immediately, but didn't say so; she just started eating again.

"Who said that?"

She shrugged. "She was joking."

"Would Andy think it's a joke?"

"Would Andy think what's a joke?"

They looked up to see Andy, plate in hand, slip into the empty seat across the table. "Hello, Bea. Hello, Martin. Nice to see you again. These pancakes look great. What joke?"

Beamer felt flushed and looked to see if perhaps several hundred more people had just crowded around their table. She wanted out. Then she looked again at Andy. He hadn't combed his hair, and the curls were crushed to one side. The urge to leave vanished.

"I'm glad you came," she said softly.

He grinned at her, then turned to Martin. "She assured me last night that I wouldn't be intruding on the two of you if I came. I hope you don't mind."

"Of course not. You look like you just got up."

"Do I?"

Beamer speared a sausage from Andy's plate and took a bite. "You do look a bit sleepy."

"I was up late. Writing a letter."

Beamer's stomach twisted.

Martin sipped coffee. "To your congressman?"

"A former girlfriend."

Beamer sat erect, but her spirits slumped. She didn't want to talk about this.

Martin leaned forward. "That's interesting."

"No, it's not," snapped Beamer.

Martin looked at Andy, who was looking at Beamer. She ate some more sausage.

"No," said Martin, "I guess it's not. Hey, isn't that Sandra, the Mad Bomber?"

Andy laughed, Beamer elbowed Martin, and they all turned to watch Sandra, Daryl, and their girls get in line for pancakes.

"Don't talk about her," said Beamer. "I'm sure everyone else in the room is, so we won't."

"That's loyalty," said Martin. "I like that about the Woodies. Close and loyal."

"Maybe a little too close," said Andy.

Martin laughed. "Especially when you're trying to be alone on a Saturday night, right?"

Andy managed a smile.

"God, I hate pancakes. I don't know why I came. Yes, I do. My mother made me. May I sit with you guys?" Sarah pulled a chair up to the end of the table. "Hi, Beamo, Andy. Hello, Martin. I'm Sarah, the yearbook editor. We've met a couple of times. I'm one of Beamer's very best friends. I'm sure she talks about me."

Martin nodded. "She does, but only enough to tease me." They all laughed.

"Why are you here?" said Beamer.

"My mother made me come. Her shelter gets money from the fund." Mrs. Ritchie was the director of a battered women's shelter.

"You may join us," said Martin, "but there are ground rules. Some taboo subjects."

"Such as?"

"Sandra, the Mad Bomber —"

Sarah giggled.

"— and Andy's former girlfriend."

Beamer wanted to slug him. "Stop, it, Martin." She looked at Andy. He seemed intent on his food.

"Former girlfriend?" said Sarah. "That's interesting. What's her name?"

"We don't know," said Martin.

"Allison," said Andy, still looking at his food. "I used to go with a girl named Allison."

"And now you go with Beamer," said Sarah.

Andy said nothing.

Sarah smiled at Beamer, then turned to Martin. "By any chance, Martin, do you have a motorcycle?"

"Sure do, but it's in winter storage."

Beamer rose. "I'm going back to work." Leaving her dishes for her friends to clear, she walked quickly to the serving line, angrily tied on a clean apron, and tugged on serving gloves. She slapped some pancakes onto a plate and brusquely handed it over, not hearing the warm greetings of Miss Patrick, her sixth-grade teacher. Miss Patrick moved on to the sausage.

Beamer looked out over the loud crowd. From where she stood behind the steaming platters of fresh pancakes she could see Martin and Sarah, talking and laughing conspiratorially. Andy had disappeared.

CHAPTER

· 13 ·

The day before Beamer's seventeenth birthday, Andy's mother lost control of her car on the highway while avoiding a cat. The car slid into a ditch and crumpled against a tree.

"She's going to live," said Andy when he called Beamer the next morning, "but she may need a new nose."

"Please, Andy, play it straight for once."

"Okay. Concussion, dislocated shoulder, internal bleeding, facial lacerations, broken nose. She's alert and really mad at herself. She's never liked cats, you know, and none of us can figure out why she bothered to save that one."

"It sounds awful. How are you doing?"

"I'm feeling very guilty. About your birthday. Look, Bea, I've got to be with the kids tonight. Do you mind? Dad's at the hospital, and someone's got to feed them. They're pretty scared. My grandmother is arriving later. Maybe when she gets here I can run your present over. I'm sorry, Bea."

"Oh, Andy, do you think it matters when your mother is in the hospital?"

"Well, there's always next year, right?"

"Sure. I'll expect you to fly home from college for the day. Just go take care of your family. And when you see your mom, give her my love."

She hung up the phone. A customer came to the counter, and she rang the sale without a word or a smile. She felt as if she had been dumped into a pit. A stinking pit. Her Saturday night escape from the store was something she depended on. A stinking pit.

"Figures," she muttered. "Well, happy birthday to me."

Three neighboring towns were sponsoring fishing contests that weekend and the store was busy with fishermen replenishing their bait and refreshments, replacing lost hats and mittens, smoking cigarettes, and waiting to hear the odd bit of gossip or fishing news. Beamer was netting a serving of minnows for a customer when Jenny and Martin entered the store. They stood inside the doorway, stamping their feet clear of snow and slush. Martin waved his red-mittened hands to Beamer. Beamer nodded and smiled, then lifted the heavy water- and fish-filled bait bag up to the nozzle of the oxygen tank and squirted in a measured dose of the gas. She twirled and knotted the bag, then led the customer back to the counter and rang up the sale. The man left and Beamer turned to Martin.

"Where have you been all day? I was hoping to get some skiing in during lunch break."

Jenny stepped behind the counter and put her arm

around Beamer. "Don't be so selfish. Our good friend here has been with me. Where's Carolyn? I've just got to show her our treasures."

"She's in the back. I'll buzz her." Beamer pressed a button on the counter, and in a moment her mother appeared, carrying a large cardboard box. She set it on the counter, greeted her friends, then turned to her daughter. "Do you want to put out these chips? I'll cover the register." Beamer nodded, pushed the box to the end of the counter, and started clipping bags to the wire rack.

"Carolyn, just look at the good stuff we got in town," Jenny said. She handed over a large shopping bag.

Beamer's mother opened the bag and lifted out several skeins of colored yarn. "Very nice," she said.

"Martin has convinced me that I should learn to knit," said Jenny.

"I want a sweater," said Martin. "No one has ever made me a sweater."

"Stay for supper and we'll have your first lesson," said Mrs. Flynn. "Beamer is a wonderful teacher."

"Mother . . ." said Beamer. She did not want to share her birthday with every stray cat, no matter how old a friend. And she certainly did not want to spend it teaching knitting.

"Well, no, then, but come for cake and I can get you started after that."

Jenny turned to Beamer. "Are we allowed to mention your birthday, or will you snap off this old hippie's head?"

"Go ahead."

"Happy birthday, Merry."

"Call me Beamer, Jenny."

"May I ask why Martin gets the privilege of using 'Merry'?"

Beamer looked beyond the expectant faces. Where was a customer when she needed one? "I don't know, Jenny. Maybe because he's not one of you."

Jenny gave this some thought. "No, he's not. But that's probably why we all like him so." She turned to Mrs. Flynn. "Anyway, I won't be by tonight until later. I have a date."

Mrs. Flynn opened the register and started counting bills. She eyed Jenny. "Do I know him?"

"No, you don't. He's entirely new and entirely wonderful."

Mrs. Flynn closed the register. "Well, come in back and tell me more." She picked up the stack of bills. "Martin, could you help Beamer for a while? The clerk went home sick before lunch and we have just been swamped."

As they left, a group of fishermen entered the store. For several minutes Beamer and Martin were busy heating sandwiches, fries, and cocoa in the microwave. When the customers had gone, they sat by the stove.

"So I'm not one of you."

"No, you're not."

"Is that why you find me attractive?"

"Who says I do?"

"Not even a bit?"

128

Beamer shrugged.

"I guess I won't pursue this any further. Happy birthday."

"Thank you."

"No present, I'm afraid."

"None expected."

"I only spend my money on girls who find me attractive. What did your parents give you?"

"What they always give — space."

Martin laughed. "No, really."

"I got new skis at Christmas. They're for my birthday, too."

"And from Andy?"

"Nosy, aren't you? I don't know yet."

"When are you going out?"

"I'm not."

"I thought you and Andy had plans."

"His mother was in an accident last night, and she's in the hospital. He's babysitting."

"Oh, Merry, that's too bad. Your birthday."

Beamer lifted her feet and rested them on the stove. "Feel sorry for Mrs. Reynolds, not me. Mother has been bad enough all day. She can just barely contain her pity."

"Okay, no pity."

"Martin, do you want to do something? A movie, maybe?"

Martin shook his head. "I'm sorry, Merry. I have a date."

Jenny and Mrs. Flynn returned. "Time to go," Jenny sang out. Martin rose, tapped Beamer softly on the shoulder, and followed Jenny out the door. Beamer resumed clipping chip bags.

"Jenny said that Martin has a date tonight," said Mrs. Flynn, "so I guess you won't be going out. Well, you can always join us."

Beamer smashed a fist on top of a bag of cheese curls. "Oh, great. Of course it's Saturday night and of course everyone is coming over with whatever weirdos and bums they've picked up and of course you'll drink wine and tea and listen to folk music and play charades. Like you have done every Saturday night of my life. No thanks, Mom. It's just not fun."

They closed the store at dusk. Mr. Flynn left to get Johnny at hockey practice. Beamer refused her mother's suggestion of a card game and went to her room. She paused at the door. "I spend too much time in here," she said, then stepped inside and lay on the bed. She was still lying down when her father and Johnny returned, and Beamer listened while her brother reported on his afternoon, her mother exclaimed about his new cuts and bruises, her father prepared supper. "There is this void," she whispered. "This huge, dark void between my life with my family and their friends and my life the way I would like it to be. All these people — I wish someone would explain them to me. Better yet, I wish someone or something would come and change it all. Just make them all go away. Or take me away."

130

After a while Beamer rose from her bed and went to the kitchen. She put her arm around her father. "Oh, yuck, Dad. Tofu ravioli?"

He stopped grating cheese. "You like it. You have always liked it."

"It's my birthday, right?"

"Right."

"Then let's all go to Bernie's Club and eat steaks."

Her family froze while considering this minor rebellion. The phone rang, releasing everyone from having to respond. Beamer answered. It was Sarah.

"Hey, Beamer, is it true you're not going out with Andy tonight?"

"True. Didn't you hear about his mother?"

"Sure, but it's your birthday, and now that you are the only woman in his life you can demand something special."

"Sarah, the poor woman is half dead."

"You need cheering up."

"I'm plenty cheerful." She grinned at her father, who was watching her as he crumbled dried herbs into the tomato sauce.

"Well, anyway, you're not going to sit alone on your birthday. What about gorgeous Martin?"

"He's doing something. Typically, involving women."

"I told you long ago to make your move."

"Move to California, that's what I'd like to do."

"So do you have any plans?"

"The Woodies will be here."

"Oh, great, plotting revolution again? Forget that. Jessie and I will be by at six. Don't eat supper."

Beamer hung up the phone. "Plans have changed," she said. "We can skip the steaks." She paused a moment before leaving the kitchen, eying each of her parents as if to dare them to ask something, anything: What plans? What friends? What party? Who's driving? They seldom asked; the family had rules, and it was assumed that she would observe them. She closed the kitchen door behind her and retreated to her room.

CHAPTER
·14·

Jessie's car flew out of the bait shop parking lot, swerved a bit on a patch of ice, then straightened. Beamer rested her head against the cold glass of the car window. "What's the plan?" she said.

The others laughed. "Just wait, just wait," said Sarah.

"I'm hungry."

"Be patient. There's a lot to look forward to."

Jessie turned up the volume of the radio. "Turn it down," said Sarah. "I hate that song."

"Tina Turner? She's great!"

"She's older than my mother."

Jessie turned off the radio and the conversation drifted along to new couples, college applications, the new biology teacher, and Pat Lambert's expulsion from school for drinking in the locker room. Beamer relaxed. She was soothed by the talk, her girlfriends' energy, the night speeding by.

The car pulled into the well-lighted and crowded parking lot of a country tavern. Beamer knew it only by its suspect reputation.

"Tinker's Tavern? Come on, you guys, I don't drink."

Sarah turned and made a face. "The entire population of the high school knows you don't drink. Don't worry, we're not here to drink."

"What then?"

Jessie pointed out the window. "Culture."

Beamer looked at a large sign. BEEFCAKE BONANZA, 9 MEN 9, TONIGHT ONLY! she read. She slumped in her seat. "Oh, no. Strippers."

They climbed out of the car and joined the throng crowding the still–closed entrance.

"They'll never let us in," said Beamer. "Don't you have to be twenty-one?"

"No problem," said Sarah. "My cousin's boyfriend Paul is the bouncer at the door. He told me this afternoon that he'd wave us right through, but that we had better not try to order beer."

Beamer felt a tug on her elbow. She turned to face Wendy.

"Happy birthday!" Wendy exclaimed. "I didn't think you'd come, but Sarah said you would, and I said you wouldn't, and I was wrong!" She dropped the cigarette that had been burning low between her gloved fingers and ground it into the snow with her foot. "This will be fun."

Beamer shrugged. "I'm not convinced."

"Just what do we do if we see any of our teachers here?" asked Jessie.

Sarah shrieked. "Can you imagine? Miss Harold?"

"Or old Frigid Farley?" said Wendy.

"Or," Jessie said, lowering her voice, "what about our mothers?"

They grinned at one another. The door opened then and the many women moved as one toward it. "Not my mother," said Beamer as the crowd surged, sucking her and the others into the tavern. "She's home eating tofu."

They were nodded through by Paul, and they quickly found an empty table.

"This is good," said Sarah. "It's not too close to the front. If we make fools of ourselves, we don't want everyone behind us watching."

"I sincerely doubt that anyone will be watching us," replied Jessie.

"Food," said Beamer. "I need food. You told me not to eat."

Wendy handed her a menu. "That's because the sandwiches here are great. You eat, we pay. Happy birthday."

"Do you come here often?"

"Bart likes it. There's usually a pretty good band playing."

"Bart? Who's Bart?"

Sarah signaled for a waitress. "Where have you been, Beamo? She's been dating him since October."

"Dating?" said Jessie. "Ha! There are other words for what she's doing with Bart."

"Beamo, ignore what you hear," said Wendy. "Try the roast beef."

"Whoa," said Jessie. "No meat for Beamer."

"Oh, that's right."

"Where have *you* guys been?" said Sarah. "Beamo here is the hot dog queen of Grand River. In the past year she has been eating meat like a prehistoric carnivore."

"I'll have the roast beef," Beamer said to the waitress. "And a Coke." The others ordered sandwiches and soft drinks.

"You know, Beamer," said Sarah, "I never could figure out how a vegetarian could run a bait shop. Isn't that just dealing in dead animals?"

"Hey, not our bait. It's fresh."

"But you're promoting the killing of fish, aren't you?"

"True. But after years of soul-searching my parents decided that eating fish was okay. For other people, that is. Their diet is still pure soybeans and nuts."

"What's the difference between eating a fish and eating a cow?"

Beamer shrugged. "They're the first to admit that their philosophy isn't pure. We all just make our choices, I guess."

Wendy grabbed Beamer's arm and pointed at the stage, where a trio of dancers had appeared. "And my choice," she said, "is the one on the left."

With the first gyration the crowd roared and began a ceaseless, rhythmic hand-clapping. Beamer munched her meal and watched the dancers. The music was loud, the costumes brief, the guys young, oiled, and good-looking. "That's not dancing," she whispered to Wendy during one number. "He's just doing aerobics." Wendy shushed her, then shouted out a lewd

136

invitation to the dancer that was lost in the general uproar. Beamer turned to Jessie, who seemed to be the only one besides herself maintaining a sense of decorum. "Are they going to strip?"

"Later, I think. They want the crowd in a frenzy first."

"A frenzy? What do they call this? Oh, no, look at that!" she said as two women rushed the stage and reached for a dancer, who adroitly wiggled away.

During the first intermission Beamer questioned Wendy about Bart. "Well, who is he and how did you meet him?"

"He graduated from Pine Grove last year and is going to the community college. We met at a party last fall at the park."

"Is it serious?"

"We're serious about having fun."

Martin's philosophy. Beamer considered it while sipping her soda slowly. The ice had melted, which watered down the flavor. She made a face.

Wendy laughed. "Look at her — she has to think about having fun." Wendy shook her head. "Loosen up, Bea. A little pleasure would do you no harm. And it doesn't look like your chances for that are good with Andy."

Beamer didn't want to talk about Andy. "Back to Bart," she said. "I don't understand it — you've been going with a guy for four months and I don't even know about it."

Wendy lit a cigarette. "That's because, dear girl, if you are not off someplace being chaste with Saint

Andrew, you're playing with that friend of yours —
the one on the radio."

"Martin."

"Yes, Marvelous Martin. No one ever sees you anymore. You play softball during lunch hour, you take
the first bus home after school, and you hide on the
weekends."

Beamer rubbed her eyes. The cigarette smoke was
thick and irritating. "I'm not that bad."

"You are that bad. Of course, if I were dividing my
time between two boys, no one would ever see me
either."

Jessie wrapped ice cubes in a cocktail napkin and
handed them to Beamer. "Here, hold this against your
eyes. It cools the burning."

"Don't bother her about Martin," said Sarah. "She
assures me it's a platonic relationship."

"Is it?" asked Jessie.

The melting ice soaked the napkin and started dripping down Beamer's wrist. She opened her eyes and
blinked. The burning was gone. "Yes," she said. "It
is very platonic and very innocent."

"I bet," said Wendy. "Innocent with Martin like
it's innocent with Andy."

Wendy had put her burning cigarette in an ashtray
next to Beamer, who pushed it across the table and
waved away the column of smoke. "It is innocent,
Wendy," she said. *Nothing you'd understand, of
course,* she added silently.

Wendy picked up her cigarette, inhaled, and released a series of small rings. "Then you're a fool."

Beamer was relieved when the music resumed. She'd never actually liked Wendy.

Two numbers into the second set, Wendy rushed to the stage and held up a five-dollar bill. The dancer grabbed the bill and placed it between his lips, then unsnapped the leather-and-rhinestone side snaps of his silk briefs. He tossed the briefs into the audience. The audience increased its roar and speeded the pace of its clapping. A G-string. Beamer wondered if it was called something different on a guy. Maybe a G-thong? The dancer sashayed toward the edge of the stage, turned his back to the crowd, untied the string, and waved it above his head as he quickly exited. The audience erupted.

Beamer slumped in her seat. She felt a tap on her shoulder and turned to Jessie.

"Do you want to leave?" Jessie said. "I'd like to. Sarah can get a ride with Wendy." Beamer nodded and they rose and left, their exit scarcely noticed by their friends.

Outside, they quickly walked to Jessie's car. Beamer inhaled deeply; the sharp, cold air was immediately and thoroughly cleansing. "I've never done it," she said, "but I think now I understand the attraction of jumping naked into a snowbank after a sauna."

"It really was hot in there. What should we do now?"

"How about a thick, cruel malt at Simpson's Café?"

"I don't think so. It's awards night for the fishing tournament, and the place will be packed with lonely fishermen."

"Sounds dangerous. Well, if you don't mind eating carob and nut cake and listening to old hippies playing children's games, we can go to my place."

"Can't be any worse than what we've just seen."

"Okay, we'll party at the bait shop."

Beamer repressed a moan as she sat on the frigid car seat. When Jessie started the car, the cold air stored in the heat vents burst out, rushing over their feet and across their faces.

"Why do we live in this cold place?" said Jessie. "It's so inhuman."

Beamer stuffed her hands deeper into her pockets. "A naked guy," she said. "Jessie, do you realize I've just seen my first naked guy?"

"Happy birthday, Beamer. Happy birthday."

CHAPTER

·15·

The highway out of town was deserted. Jessie fiddled with the radio, finally pulling in a distant southern station. They listened to the strong, clear sound for several minutes before speaking.

"Carob, that's a substitute for chocolate, right? So your family doesn't eat chocolate either?" Jessie's voice was politely incredulous.

"I'm exaggerating. They gave in years ago and started eating chocolate again."

"You always make fun of the commune. I can't believe you hated it that much. What was it like?"

"The commune?"

"Yeah."

"It was pretty. Woodlands must have been the most beautiful spot in northern Minnesota. Still is, even though they've built those townhouses and tennis courts."

"That's not what I meant. What was it like living there?"

Beamer took off her mittens and stuffed them into her jacket pockets. "Crowded. Maybe not literally, but it felt that way. There were people everywhere. If I went walking in the woods, there was someone there. If I went to the beach, someone was there. Everywhere. We lived in this dorm, kind of a cabin, really —"

"Like the one by the picnic spot?"

"That's the very one. Twelve of us lived in that dorm."

"Twelve people, wow."

"And that was after they built the other dorms. For about two years everyone was together. Let me tell you, you can crowd a lot of bunk beds into one building. I was conceived in a bunk bed."

Jessie laughed. "It does sound crowded."

"It wasn't just the living conditions, it was knowing that no matter what I did, people were watching. Everything. When I was eight I wanted to join the Brownies. They took a vote! All of them. My parents couldn't just decide that for themselves; they all had to vote. That's what I really mean by crowded."

"Did they let you join?"

"No. They decided the Scouts were too militaristic. Those brown uniforms, I guess."

Jessie laughed, shifted slightly in her seat, and changed her grip on the steering wheel. "At least you were never lonely."

Beamer turned to look out the window. "I'm not so sure," she said softly.

They let a mile speed by. The radio station was playing another Tina Turner song. The girls looked at each other and smiled.

"She's older than my mother too," said Beamer.

The rough beat of the song kept pace with the speeding car. Beamer closed her eyes and nodded along. The song was on the jukebox at Simpson's Café, and she and Andy had often danced to it. "You know, Jessie, this may come as a surprise, but Andy is a terrific dancer."

"I've noticed. We've all noticed. And we've also all noticed that you are the only one he ever, ever dances with. He's a nice guy, Beamo. You're lucky. Too bad about tonight, though."

"He is a nice guy. And of course, if I had been with Andy tonight I would not, definitely not, have seen a naked guy."

"You guys have been going out for — what?"

"Six months. Steady and true."

"And still no sex?"

"No."

"Everyone knows about his famous statement, of course, but we were all so quick to laugh that no one asked him why. Can you tell me why he doesn't want to? Religious reasons?"

"No. It would be nice if it were that clear."

"Why, then?"

Beamer drew a long breath. *He does want to,* she thought, but didn't say. "Waiting isn't a strict rule for him, okay? He just thinks it might be a good idea."

"A good idea for others?"

"For anybody."

"If it's not an absolute, why not?"

Beamer shrugged.

"No suspicions? You two must at least talk about it."

"A little."

"So?"

"What can I say? All year he's been staying in touch with his old girlfriend. And sometimes I think he was avoiding even talking about sex because he was confused about commitments."

"Sarah told me he broke off with her."

"I'll kill her."

"Who?"

"Sarah. She's got such a mouth."

"So if Andy's not confused anymore, what happens next? More talk, or will he push for something else?"

Their warm breath had fogged over the side windows. Beamer traced a heart and inscribed it with her own and Andy's initials. "True love always," she said. Jessie laughed.

"Andy would never, ever force anything," Beamer said.

"Of course not. So it's mostly you saying no."

"Mostly."

"Why?"

Beamer didn't answer.

"Everybody who's doing it says it's pretty special."

Beamer shrugged. "So they say."

"You doubt it?"

Beamer thought of Wendy, of the women screaming after the strippers; she thought of Martin and his long list of girls. "Jessie, I truly believe that without anything meaningful in life, yeah, sex probably seems special. I suppose it could fill some emptiness."

Jessie laughed. Beamer looked at her and frowned.

"I'm sorry, Beamo. What you said is really great. I think you're right. I laughed because, well, most of us have fears about sex, or ideas about sex. You have a philosophy."

Beamer smiled. "It's how I was raised. Life itself is a philosophy."

"So tell me, is there a simple reason why you don't want to have sex with Andy?"

With a slow circular motion of her palm, Beamer erased the heart. "I guess I just don't want to be that close to someone."

They reached the store. "Thanks for letting me intrude on something so private," Jessie said.

"No big deal."

"It was always an issue between Rob and me, which might explain why once again I was free and single on a Saturday night."

"I'm glad you were. Rob's loss." They got out of the car and walked toward the store. "Jessie," said Beamer as she reached to open the door, "I feel like I should warn you about this."

"About what?"

"These people are kind of weird about my birthday. I was the first baby born at the commune, and they have always celebrated my birthday. With or without me."

"That's weird? It just sounds sweet."

"No, it's not sweet, it's like —" She gripped the doorknob tightly, but didn't turn it. "— it's like they can't let go of something that isn't there."

"I think it's sweet."

Beamer sighed. "Let's see if there's any cake left."

Their entrance went unnoticed. A small circle of the friends were engaged in earnest conversation around the wood stove. Beamer led Jessie to the back room, where they deposited their coats, then up the stairs to the family's home. They met Maud going down. Beamer introduced Jessie.

"Wonderful," said Maud. "We're about to start charades and can use some more people. Will you join us?"

"Probably not," said Beamer.

"Maybe after we have some cake," said Jessie.

Maud sobered. "Oh," she said. "Oh, no."

"Did you eat all my birthday cake?" Beamer demanded.

"Not me personally," said Maud. "But yes, it's gone."

Beamer turned to Jessie. "Do you think that's sweet?"

Jessie was smiling. "Yes, I do."

The kitchen was crowded. Beamer introduced Jessie to the Woodies nearest at hand. Mrs. Flynn was administering first aid to Sue's hand, cut deeply in a fruit-slicing accident. Mr. Flynn was reading through some papers, Peter at his elbow. Beamer smiled at her father and peered over his shoulder. Peter was a well-known writer of nature essays. He often brought his work

146

to Mr. Flynn for informal editing. Beamer plowed through a cluster of friends in earnest conversation, something, she gathered, about groundwater purity and the paper company. She filled two mugs with cocoa from a carafe, then retreated.

She found Jessie talking to Jenny in the hall outside the kitchen.

"No, Ms. Elliot, I haven't gotten the test results."

Jenny was stern. "Call me Jenny, Jessie. We're at the bait shop, not in the classroom."

Jessie nodded. "I'll try."

"Wrong, Ms. Elliot," said Beamer. "You're not in either place. You are in my home, about twenty feet from my room, which is where I'd like to go with my friend. If you don't mind. Anyway, didn't you have a date tonight?"

"Oh, he's here somewhere."

Maud reappeared from downstairs. "Game time," she called out. She grabbed Jenny and Jessie by their elbows. "You two are on my team." Beamer frowned. She did not want to end the day this way.

Jessie sipped cocoa, looked at Beamer, then shook her head. "Thanks, but no. I want to talk with Bea a bit more, then get home."

Maud made a face. "First Andy, now Jessie. Evidently Moonbeam selects her friends according to their ability to resist fun."

"Oh, we had fun earlier tonight," said Jessie.

"Doing what?" Mrs. Flynn took up position in the doorway behind Beamer.

Beamer sipped cocoa. "Ate supper, came home."

Jessie held her mug in front of her smile.

Maud shook her head. "No fun." She and Jenny and a line of others filed downstairs to the store.

Beamer turned to her mother. "What did Maud mean about Andy?"

"You missed him. He came by with his sisters and stayed for about an hour. The girls played cards with the other children and Andy visited with us."

"And helped eat all the cake," said Jessie with a wide smile.

Mrs. Flynn frowned. "Oh, yes. You heard about the cake."

"You ate all my cake."

"Every last crumb. You should have stayed home. Jessie, will you join us downstairs? Beamo hates it, but you look more reasonable."

Jessie laughed. "I'm heading home, Mrs. Flynn, but maybe another time."

"That's what Andy said. He's never yet played charades with us, but tonight we got him to promise to come back with his family as soon as his mother is well."

Beamer groaned. "Not really?"

"Yes, really. Goodnight, Jessie. Drive carefully. Oh, Bea, Andy left your present in your room."

Jessie lifted Beamer's empty mug from her hand and carried it to the kitchen. She returned and nudged Beamer toward the stairs. "I should get going, Bea."

The back room was empty. Jessie pulled her coat from the pile that had tumbled onto the floor.

"Does this go on every Saturday night?"

"Usually."

"Fun."

Beamer shrugged.

Jessie sat next to her on the sofa. "I live alone with my mother, Beamer. I hardly ever hear from my father, and my brothers come home maybe twice a year. This seems so wonderful to me, a house full of people. All these friends."

"It can be nice."

"But crowded, right?"

Beamer nodded. "Sometimes, Jessie, I just feel smothered."

Jessie zipped her coat. "Too bad you missed Andy."

"Sounds like I wouldn't have had a chance to talk with him anyway. They do that — anyone I bring in, they grab away." She pointed a finger at Jessie. "They almost got you."

"Charades with a bunch of forty-year-olds; don't tell anyone I nearly gave in."

"The entire night will be one solemn secret, I promise."

Jessie opened the door to the cold. "Oh, and Beamo —"

"Yeah?"

"He was my first naked guy too."

Beamer watched while Jessie drove carefully out of the parking lot, then onto the highway. The car accelerated and quickly disappeared. Beamer debated joining the Woodies, then remembered Andy's gift. She ran up the steps and into her room. The parking-lot lights flooded through the window, casting broad shadows. She scanned the room for a package. A long narrow box lay on her pillow. She prepared for bed before opening the gift, then sat down and unwrapped it. It was one of his own pottery pieces — a long, elegant, narrow vase with a perfect blue glaze and delicate white brushstrokes. She stroked the smooth surface, then placed it carefully on the table by her bed. She opened the card, and peered hard to read in the dark. Frustrated, she lit a candle.

It was a short, scribbled message:

> Happy birthday. I'd love to give you something special, but I'm not sure what that could be. This will have to do.

Beamer lay down under her comforter, the card in her hand. She suspected Andy wasn't just talking about the vase and his art. She touched the vase again and wondered about next year, when he would be at art school in Rhode Island. She wondered if he would write; she wondered if he would call; she wondered how much it would hurt if he didn't.

A wave of applause signaled the end of a charade. The voices and other noise meant the friends were going home. The door slammed a number of times, but no cars started. *They're hiking across the lake to look at the stars,* she thought, and she considered dressing and joining the excursion. Just as she reached for her jeans, a barrage of snowballs assaulted her window, and then the assembled Woodies stood below and sang "Happy Birthday."

Beamer opened the window, shoving hard against the seal of ice and packed snow. "I hope you all know that every one of you is getting gray hair. And it looks awful."

"We love you too, Beamo," shouted Maud. Beamer waved, then closed the window. One by one the cars started and left.

She propped the note against the vase, blew out the candle, and quickly fell asleep.

CHAPTER
· 16 ·

It was an old dream, her oldest, really her very first memory disguised in sleep. Once a nightmare that had caused her to scream and run to her parents' arms, it was now so familiar that when it returned she seldom did more than stir slightly and roll to a cooler spot on the pillow.

As in a bad book or movie, the battle lines were clear: the sheriff and townspeople hated those crazy Chicago hippies who'd bought all that good land by the big lake and turned it into a commune. And who knew for sure what kind of things they were doing out there?

One morning the sheriff drove into Woodlands. He was followed by two pickups and a van. Five A.M.; only Daniel and Peter were up. The sheriff flashed a warrant. "Let's see what drugs you've got out here. Let's clean things up," he said. Then he got the dogs. Loud dogs, big dogs. Two dogs scratching and leaping and bouncing off the walls of the van.

The dogs woke everyone. Beamer sat straight up on her small mattress on the floor and looked directly into the snarling face of a dog big enough to eat a three-year-old. Still only two, she started to cry. Her father lifted her and carried her outside, where they waited with the silent, watchful group while the men and dogs searched. Beamer lifted her head from her father's shoulder and saw a dog leave the building, its teeth sunk into her soft, worn rag doll. The dog shook its head and the trailing ends of the doll's gingham dress whipped back and forth in the dewy grass.

There were no drugs, never had been, never would be. No people engaged in group sex, no witchcraft. The sheriff left, certain he had done the right thing, uncertain what to do next. The Woodies consulted quickly, standing outside in their nightclothes. Dogs, even! What should they do?

Beamer, released by her father, ran through the grass to retrieve her doll. She picked it up, then threw it back on the ground. It smelled — it smelled like a dog.

"I don't ever want a dog," Beamer said to Andy. "No dogs, ever."

The hospital intercom crackled a doctor's name; an aide rushed by with a serving cart; a pair of somber-looking women passed. Andy tugged on Beamer's arm, then directed her toward a vinyl sofa. They sat down.

"Okay, no dogs. Just a few kids and a station wagon, right?"

Beamer smiled. "Just no dogs. Do you want to know why?"

Andy slouched down until his head was level with her shoulder, then he leaned against her. Beamer took his hand and tucked it under her arm. "Do you want to know why?" she repeated.

"No."

Beamer pushed his hand away and rose. "That's sweet. I want to share one of my oldest fears and you're not interested. I guess I'll go see your mother now." She took two steps, then turned back to face him, still slouched on the sofa. "Martin would be interested. I'll save it for him."

Mrs. Reynolds was sitting up in bed, examining a large drawing her daughters had brought.

"It's for the wall in here, Mom," Kim said.

"Put it somewhere you can see it," advised Julie.

"Oh, here's Beamer," said Mrs. Reynolds, laying the drawing down. "Hello, dear. And happy birthday." The girls chorused a greeting.

"Hi, Mrs. Reynolds." Beamer stepped to the foot of the bed. "I hope you're feeling better." She took a small wrapped box from her coat pocket and handed it to Andy's mother. "For your quick recovery."

"Beamer, how sweet! And after I ruined your birthday."

Out of the corner of her eye, Beamer saw Andy slink into the room.

154

"You didn't ruin a thing. I had a great time. Just don't ask me what I did." Mrs. Reynolds and her daughters laughed.

"That good, huh?" said Kim.

Julie sat on her mother's bed, bouncing a little as she settled in. Mrs. Reynolds moaned softly, but put her arm around her daughter.

"Geez, Julie, get off, would you? Be smart," Andy snapped.

Beamer turned and looked at Andy, taking in his stony face. He didn't look at her. *Oh boy,* she thought, *one remark about Martin and I've ruined his day.*

"Oh, look at these!" Mrs. Reynolds exclaimed as she opened her gift. She lifted out two thick red slippers with snowflake designs on the toes. "Beamer, you made these, didn't you? This is the same yarn you used for Andy's scarf. They're lovely."

"They're for keeping your feet warm while you recover by the fireside and the men in the house take care of you."

"Well, if that happens, then this accident will have been a good thing."

Everybody laughed at that, and Andy stepped to the bed and examined the socks. His face as he turned to Beamer had cheered, and he smiled at her.

"Andy and Beamer, look at the picture the girls did for me," said Mrs. Reynolds, handing over the drawing. Beamer laughed at the sketch, a cartoon depiction of a cat being chased off the road by Mrs. Reynolds, who was safely motoring in an army tank.

"Cats," Andy's mother said, shaking her head. "I can't stand them. Give me a good dog any day."

Andy and Beamer smiled at each other. "Not me," said Andy. "I don't ever want a dog."

"Beamer, please sit down," said Mrs. Reynolds.

"I can't stay. I just wanted to stop in and see how you were."

"And see Andy," said Kim, and she and her sister giggled.

"Did you like the vase he gave you for your birthday?" asked Julie.

"Yes, it's beautiful. I've told him that at least twenty times." Beamer stepped to the side of the bed, took Mrs. Reynold's hand, and squeezed it gently. "My mom said to let us know if you need help with anything. I've gotta go now. Rest easy."

Andy's mother leaned back against her pillow. "Thank you, dear."

Beamer tapped Kim and Julie each lightly on the arm, then left the room. Andy caught up with her at the elevator. He put his arm around her, then dropped it when they were joined by other people. They didn't speak until they reached the car.

Andy held open the car door while Beamer started the engine and buckled up.

"We could go somewhere for lunch. My treat."

"I should get back to the store."

"Okay," he said. "I'm sorry. Obviously I'm guilty of some terrible insensitivity. So please tell me now why you don't like dogs."

156

Beamer peeled off a glove and held her hand over the heat vent. "This heater is lousy," she said. "I'll be frozen by the time I get home."

"Tell me."

She pulled the door closed, then rolled down the window. He leaned in and kissed her on the cheek. "Tell me about the dog thing," he said.

"It's nothing, really," she said. "Just something that happened a long time ago. I dreamed about it last night. That's why I brought it up."

"Thanks for coming. My mom likes you a lot, you know."

"And mine likes you."

"I know. We had a good talk last night. Maybe some Saturday we should just skip the movie or whatever's going on and stay at the bait shop. It was pretty much fun there last night. Sure cheered the girls up. We could —"

"Andy, that is the last thing I want to do on a Saturday night. The last, the last —"

"Bea, okay. You're clear, I hear you."

A car pulled into the spot next to them. The doors opened and a family spilled out onto the snow-packed lot.

"Bea —"

Two of the boys from the car shoved each other and bumped Andy. "You take the stupid flowers," one shouted. "Forget it!" shouted his brother. They pushed each other toward the hospital.

"Bea, I love you."

Beamer sighed while something twisted inside. She watched the family walk away, the boys still scuffling. "I do, you know that."

She knew what he wanted to hear, but she kept still, kept her eyes on the family until they disappeared into the building.

She looked at him. "I know that. I'll see you in the morning." She shifted and drove away.

Beamer blocked Andy out of her mind. She drove fast and sang along with the radio and kept her eyes and thoughts on the empty road. She had forgotten her sunglasses, so she drove with eyes squinted against the glare. She hadn't planned it, hadn't really thought of him since the day before, but when Martin's road appeared — a small tree-lined chute into the woods — she slowed and turned.

He was surprised to see her. "I'm working, but come in for a little while."

Beamer paused. *How weird is this?* she thought. *My boyfriend tells me he loves me, and I drive straight to Martin.* "Not if you're working. I'll go." She didn't move.

"Actually, I'm glad you're here. I want you to listen to a tape." He took hold of her arm and pulled her in. "I went out on an interview this morning, and it was great. There's this maternity home in Grand River, did you know that?"

"I've only lived here all my life, Martin."

"That means yes, I suppose."

"Pregnant girls, Martin? That's what you want me to listen to?"

He nodded. "It's the best interview I've done. I hardly said a thing, they just talked all morning."

Beamer listened to the interview tape while Martin made tea. Several times she punctuated the girls' confessions, sobs, and dreams with snorts and groans. "Stupid girls," she said at one point.

Martin stopped the tape. "Cut it out, okay? Just because you uphold a doctrine of chastity doesn't mean you can sneer at others."

"It's not the sex, Martin. I can handle that. I don't agree with it, but I can handle it."

"So why call them stupid?"

"It was a bad word to use."

"What bothered you?"

"Losing control of your life, that bothers me."

Martin eyed her thoughtfully.

"Did you hear what they were saying? 'I had the baby for him'; 'I know he still loves me'; 'I would go home if he would only write.' I don't like that, Martin."

"That they care about someone?"

"No, that caring makes them give up control. They've let someone come in and take over."

"But what if someone comes into a girl's life and doesn't want to take over? No demands, no changes. He just wants to enjoy being there. Is that different?"

Beamer considered her answer. And as she did, she thought, finally, of Andy, remembering his suggestion to settle in on a Saturday night at the bait shop and recalling his pleading look when he had said, "I love you." She shook the picture away and looked at

Martin. His usually teasing eyes were still and clear. He rubbed his unshaven face with the back of his hand. She could almost feel the roughness.

"That might be different," she said softly, "if it were possible."

He smiled again. "I agree. Completely." He rose. "Would you like some pie? I've got half an apple pie waiting to be eaten."

"I haven't had lunch yet, Martin."

"Consider it lunch."

"Okay, a small piece."

"I have to wash forks. I guess I haven't done dishes for some time."

"I can do that."

"Just sit down. It will only take a minute."

She pulled a chair from the table, moved to sit, then hesitated. She lifted a woman's sweater from the chair and held it up.

"This is interesting, Martin. I didn't know you wore lavender."

He came to the table with the pie and some clean, wet silverware. "We built too big a fire and it got hot."

Beamer snickered. "I bet it did."

"Merry, do you want pie or do you want to be obnoxious? I'll send you home in that case."

"I'll be nice," she said sweetly. They both sat down.

"It's not anyone you know."

"Not interested, Martin."

"She knows you, though. Or about you. Of course, most people do, after Rae Ramone's story."

"I don't want to be sent home, Martin, so I don't want to talk about her."

"Now I'm talking about you."

"Don't. Just eat."

They finished, then sat down by the fire with fresh mugs of tea.

"How was the quiet birthday with the Woodies?"

"I went out with friends."

"Good."

"We went to the male dance show at Tinker's Tavern."

Martin's eyes grew round. "Strippers? Did you enjoy yourself?"

"No. Jessie Waverly and I left early and went back to the bait shop."

Martin laughed. "You left early and went home? And did what? Played charades, I bet. Oh, Merry, couldn't you let loose for even one night?" He shook his head. "You are so different from the other girls I know."

"How so?"

"I'm not sure. Just different."

"Different from Katie?" She had learned the name of his old girlfriend from Jenny.

Martin raised his teacup to his lips, then lowered it. "We don't talk about Andy, do we?"

"No."

"Well, then."

"Fair enough."

"Thank you."

"Well, what can we talk about? The weather?"

He looked out the window. "It's started to snow."

"Skiing could be perfect in a little while. Are you interested?"

"I need to work. I want this interview to be perfect. I'm going to submit it with my application for a summer internship in Washington."

"D.C.?"

"Yup. National Public Radio. They always take on some fools who will work for nothing and die while they're doing it. I want to be one of them."

Martin's cat attacked Beamer's lap. While she calmed it with some ear scratching, she digested the news of his plans. He'd be going away. She had always assumed he would; this wasn't his home. Still, the stated fact was unpleasant.

"I'll miss you," she said. "You've been good company this winter."

"Come with me."

She looked startled.

"I mean it. A bunch of us will be renting a townhouse. You could get a job somewhere. It would do you good to get away from the bait shop. The parties will be great, I promise."

"Is that supposed to make me want to go? Great parties?"

He laughed. "I forgot you're not a party animal. Well, the museums are nice."

"I doubt if Mom and Dad would let me go. Besides, it sounds too adventurous. I'll stick with the minnows." She rose, went to the table, and carried their

162

dirty dishes to the kitchen. When she returned, Martin rose to meet her. He held her firmly, then kissed her gently.

She pulled back. "Don't."

He smiled. "Just a whim, Merry. Just a friendly whim."

"We're friends, Martin. I'm not someone to add to your long list of cabin conquests."

"Merry, it was a friendly kiss. And you're not on any list. No one is."

"Sarah says —"

"Sarah doesn't know me."

Beamer fingered the edge of the table.

"Merry, don't hate me for having fun. I was serious and steady with one person for a long, long time. And now it's over. And if I want to keep busy looking around, well, don't hate me."

"I don't hate you." She pointed to the lavender sweater. "So tell me her name."

"Merry, I'm not trying to hide anything, but her name doesn't mean anything."

"Even to you?"

He started to protest, then reconsidered. "Maybe not. Do you think that's awful?"

"Meaningless sex?"

"It is never meaningless. Call it uncommitted."

"Martin, I was raised by people whose every breath was a commitment. Yes, I think it is wrong."

He tilted his head to the side. "But is it appealing? Maybe just a little?"

"It's wrong," she said quietly.

Martin shook his head. "You are going to be a terrific mother someday."

"What an awful thing to say."

"But it's so true. Time for you to go home. I have work to do."

He walked with her to the car. She got in, buckled the seatbelt, and started the engine, then rolled down the window. "I'd like to hear the tape when you've finished editing it," she said. "I promise not to laugh and sneer."

He nodded. "I'll drop off a copy. And forget about the kiss. It didn't mean a thing." He waved, then turned and ran back into the cabin. Beamer sat for a moment in the still car. The fast-falling snow had entirely blanketed the windows; the stillness and the silence were complete.

One boy says he loves me, she thought, *and the other kisses me and says it doesn't mean a thing.* She exhaled sharply, and the sudden burst of moist air fogged a large patch on the windshield. She tapped the wiper switch and watched the wipers stroke across the windshield, revealing a thick wall of falling snow. As she carefully guided the car along the narrow road, Beamer wiped the fog patch on the glass with her glove and made a face. Nothing seemed any clearer.

CHAPTER

·17·

Just as she neared home plate, Beamer felt her feet slipping out from underneath her. As her body followed her feet into a liftoff from the icy path, she twisted in midair and reached for the plate. The fielder's throw whizzed by and died in a snowbank. Beamer was safe; she had scored a run. Her team had won the tournament.

She relished the cheers and applause. She embraced and congratulated her teammates, then looked into the crowd. Her parents waved, Johnny saluted, and Sarah, Jessie, and some other friends threw snowballs. During the brief awards ceremony she saw Andy standing with Johnny. He responded to her wave with a thumbs-up but no smile.

"Good show," he said when she joined him afterward.

"You may touch my medal," she said, "but only if your hands are clean."

Sarah and the others came by. "We're going over to the Elks' tent for hot dogs," Sarah said. "Do Romeo and Juliet want to join us?"

"No, thanks," Andy said quickly. "We're cruising the fair alone."

Beamer looked at Sarah and shrugged. "Thanks for asking." She watched her friends depart. "That would have been fun," she said.

"Sorry. I didn't feel like a party. Let's go. You promised me a guided tour of the Eighth Annual Grand River WinterFest. I want it now."

City Park covered several square blocks along the riverfront near the center of town. The park grounds sloped gently down from the softball diamond on the northern edge to the riverbank. The center of the park was a large pond, actually a backwater or lagoon of the river. The WinterFest activities were located along the sidewalk that circled the pond, and on either of the two festival days a few thousand people might be promenading.

Beamer and Andy stood at the edge of the circling mass of people.

"Everybody walks in the same direction," Andy observed.

"Clockwise," said Beamer. "It's always clockwise. I don't know why, there's no written rule, people just do it." They plunged in, and were immediately greeted by a green-haired clown who handed them each a Tootsie Roll and kissed Andy on the cheek. The clown disappeared into the crowd. They walked along.

Three jugglers started performing near the pond and the promenade thinned out. Andy and Beamer continued walking, stopping at all the commercial displays to talk with friends who were working or to accept free souvenirs. They had nearly finished the circle when Andy stopped to inspect his booty. "Seven bumper stickers, eleven balloons, two windshield scrapers, and one bookmark. What a haul."

"Wait until you get to our booth."

"What are your folks giving away?"

"The same thing they've given away every year for three years. You won't believe it when you see it."

They reached the bait shop booth. Beamer's father immediately stepped from behind the table. "Let me look at your cheek," he said to his daughter, and he carefully examined the reddened bump and scrape under her eye, the result of a second inning fielding mishap.

"Well, it looked a lot worse from the bleachers," he said. "What a dumb game."

"Dad!" Beamer protested.

"That's just what I've been saying all winter," said Andy. "She never listens, though."

Mr. Flynn smiled at Andy. "Give this boy a key chain."

"That's what we're here for," said Beamer, and she fished a handful out of a large bin. "Take enough for the family."

Andy examined one. "Oh, no," he said. "This is really awful."

The ornament of the key chain was a clear plastic rectangle with the shop's name and address printed on one side. Inside the plastic, preserved perfectly, with its mouth gaping, was a tiny minnow.

"I don't understand it," said Mrs. Flynn, "but we give away at least three thousand every festival." Mr. and Mrs. Flynn turned then to attend to other visitors. Beamer and Andy wandered off.

"I don't want to sound critical," said Andy, "but this isn't exactly the souvenir you would expect to get from committed vegetarians."

"Don't ask me to explain their philosophies. Don't ask them to."

"Is there something to watch now," he said, "or should we eat?"

Beamer thought. "Well, the snow golfing is fun, but that's almost over, I bet. Have you seen the snow sculptures?"

"Yes. I wasn't impressed."

"The snowmobile races should be starting. That's weird enough to be fun."

"What's so weird about it? They have them every weekend."

"This is different. They race over the pond."

"But it's mostly open water."

"That's right."

Andy stopped walking and was immediately bumped from behind. The person swore and passed. Beamer grabbed his elbow and pulled him along. "They race their snowmobiles on water?"

She nodded. "They go one—on—one. They start on snow, race along a twenty-foot path, then hit open water. It's about a thousand feet across to solid ground. Some of them don't make it."

"I don't understand."

"They try to race their machines across open water. By momentum, mostly. The driver often ends up swimming to shore. The snowmobile is marked with a little float that shows where it sank so they can tow it out."

"Grown men and women do this?"

"They even pay. There's a fifty-dollar entry fee."

Andy let out a low, soft whistle. "I think I'd rather eat some hot dogs."

They purchased their food and carried it to an empty table. As the snowmobile race began, a crowd formed near the pond, which left the booths and food stands almost empty.

"Lousy day for a picnic," Andy said. He blew on his bare fingers, then laced them around his cocoa cup.

"No, it's a perfect day. It's warm enough to be outside comfortably, but not so warm that the snow gets soft and messy. If —" The roaring sound of snowmobile engines interrupted. Andy turned and looked toward the pond.

"How can we carry on a conversation with that din?"

"You'll get used to it. There, they've stopped already." The engines were silent, but the crowd watching the race had erupted into cheers, laughter, and applause.

"Did someone just sink?"

"Probably."

Andy swore softly. "What idiots," he added.

169

"Lighten up, okay? I feel like dumping you in a pond."

A dog came and sniffed at their table. Andy prodded it with his boot. "Beat it, mutt," he said. The dog left.

"What is your problem today?" Beamer said. "I've never seen you like this. Time of the month or something?"

Andy sipped his cocoa and stared at Beamer. "My problem is you."

"What do you mean?"

"Last week when you left me at the hospital, where did you go?"

She didn't answer.

"I was watching the game with your brother today. He said he had to cover for you at the store last Sunday because you were having lunch with Martin. Is that right? You rushed away from me so you could go have lunch with him?"

"We had pie, not lunch."

"Oh, that makes a difference."

"Andy, if you are going to throw a tantrum every time I see him —"

"I don't care if you see him, as long as you see me. As long as you want to see me." His voice softened. "And I don't know if you do."

He had left a perfect opening. Beamer cautiously entered. "Actually, you're making this easy."

"What?"

"I was going to wait until later, but I guess I might as well do it now. I want to break up, Andy."

He groaned. "No."

170

"Yes."

"Why? It is Martin. I've been a fool all along, right? It's Martin? That guy has just breezed in and ruined everything."

"It's not Martin."

"Why, then?"

Beamer poked a hole in her hot dog bun with her little finger. "I just think I should care more."

"What?"

"If we're going to keep on the way we're going, I think I should care more."

"Care more? I don't buy it, Bea. All those times together, all the talks. Saying goodnight in the back of the bait shop. Don't lie to me." He leaned forward. "It's because I brought up sex, right? But we settled that. We won't."

"Andy, it has gotten to be too much. It's like you're suddenly wrapping your arms around me and instead of feeling good, it's just too damn tight."

A wind gust blew over Andy's half-empty cocoa cup. He let it lie, the cocoa dripping onto the snow.

"You've broken up with Allison and you've told me you love me. And I feel like I should do something for you. But I can't."

"It's the Woodies," he said, his words clipped.

"They have nothing to do with this, Andy."

"Maybe not directly, but they're there."

"How so?"

"Bea, you have worked so hard for so long at not loving the Woodies that now you can't even admit you love anybody. You can't throw them out of your

171

life, so instead you get rid of me." He dropped his hot dog onto his plate and drummed a quick, hard cadence on the table with his fingers. He didn't look at Beamer, who was watching him intently. "You're lying to yourself, Bea. It's a big lie."

Andy rose and walked away. Beamer stayed at the table, staring at the remains of her lunch. A raucous roar from the pond signaled the sinking of another snowmobile. She had been planning this all week. Planning what she'd say, when she'd say it, anticipating his response. It hadn't gone right, but it was done. Still, it would have been easier if he hadn't cried.

CHAPTER
· 18 ·

Beamer did not look forward to school on Monday. She called Sarah after returning home from WinterFest and announced her breakup with Andy; she was certain that everyone would know by Monday.

Everyone did, and everyone wanted details.

"There's nothing to say," Beamer said repeatedly. "We just broke up."

The heavy questioning persisted only through lunch hour; then it was old news. Beamer was eating lunch with friends in the cafeteria when she saw Andy across the crowded room. He was sitting alone, eating and staring at nothing.

Someone tapped Beamer on the shoulder. She turned and saw Josh Samuels, athlete *extraordinaire*, honor student, and tenor soloist. Josh straddled the chair next to Beamer's. "Is it all true," he said, "what I hear about you and the sensitive artist?"

"All true."

"They say you're not talking about why. I bet I know why."

"Tell me why, Josh."

"It's that Martin. Everyone has been waiting for the two of you to give up that brother-and-sister act."

"No, Josh."

He leaned closer. "Then I'll guess again. Andy came out of the closet, right? Confessed he likes boys better than he likes girls?"

Beamer leaned back in her chair. "Oh, Josh. You are such an idiot."

He shrugged. "He's a strange one, that's for sure. Anyway, what really matters is now you are free. So let's do something this weekend."

Her friends were picking up their lunch refuse and pretending not to listen. Beamer stood up. "I'm free, Josh, but not interested."

That week Beamer turned down three other boys when they suggested a movie, a party, bowling on the weekend. She said no to Sarah's suggestion that they crash a dance at the community college, and she told Wendy that she didn't think she could make it to her birthday celebration.

After classes on Friday she hurried to her bus, wanting to avoid Andy, whose last class was held near her locker. Martin was standing close to the buses. "I'm glad I caught you," he said. "Something came up with a friend at school and so I'm going to Chicago for a while."

"Anything serious?"

"Probably not. Anyway, it's a good excuse to get away. Sort of a spiritual sabbatical."

"Tell the truth now: you just can't take the cold. What about your show?"

"Elizabeth is going to substitute. Will you feed the cat? Here are my keys."

"Sure. You could have just left them at the store."

"I was in town and I wanted to say goodbye."

Beamer's bus was about to leave. Martin touched her shoulder lightly, and Beamer boarded. She watched him until he was out of sight, then sat still with her eyes closed. Winter break started Wednesday. Nearly two weeks of no school. She had been looking forward to it, but now, with Andy out of her life and Martin gone, the vacation would be empty, long and lonely.

It was a long vacation. During the days Beamer worked in the store, and at night she retreated to her room. She read, cleaned her desk, reorganized her bureau drawers, ripped down all her posters, and thought about painting the walls. She knit a cap for Johnny and started a sweater for her father.

Josh and two other boys called and asked for a date. She turned each one down. On Friday Sarah invited her to go shopping and restaurant hopping in Minneapolis for two days. Beamer said no. On Saturday Jessie suggested they go skiing. Beamer said no. On Tuesday night a carload of friends stopped at the store and urged Beamer to join them for pizza and dancing at a club in a nearby town. Beamer said she didn't feel well, and went to bed at nine.

She was finally getting sleepy at ten-thirty when her mother walked into her room.

"Don't you believe in knocking?" said Beamer.

"I read somewhere that a good clue a child is using drugs is when he never comes out of his bedroom."

"Oh."

"That's not the problem, though, is it?"

"What problem? I don't have any problem."

"Why don't you call Andy? Seems to me you miss him." Mrs. Flynn sat on the edge of the bed.

"Thanks for the advice, Mom, but you don't know anything about it."

"Enlighten me."

"And have you share my feelings and the details of my life with Peter and Sue and Jenny and Maud and every Joe Blow who stops by for a can of worms? Sorry, Mom, but this is my life and I'm holding on to it."

If she had poked her mother in the eye, the pain could not have been more obvious. Mrs. Flynn rose. "I don't think I'd do that," she said softly. "I have some sense."

Beamer sat up. "Mom, look — don't get too frantic over me. I'm okay. I'm just bored. I guess that's why I'm so sulky. If I miss anyone, it's probably Martin. He's the one I did things with this winter."

Mrs. Flynn turned slightly and light from the hall illuminated her face. Quickly and clearly concern wiped away the hurt in her expression. "Martin?" She crossed her arms, as if that act of restraint could stifle the words that were ready to come. "Well," she said

176

lightly, falsely, "if boredom is your problem, the cure for that is to do something."

"I will."

Mrs. Flynn began to leave the room, then paused. "Did he mention to you that he would be seeing his old girlfriend in Chicago? He told Jenny they'd run up a fortune in phone bills during the past few weeks. I hope it works out. Goodnight, dear." She closed the door, sealing the room in darkness.

Beamer lay back, no closer to sleep than she had been at noon. *His old girlfriend?* she thought. *Well, why not? That's fine with me. After all, Martin had nothing to do with why I broke up with Andy. I'm certain of that.* She punched her pillow into a mound. *I think.*

The next morning Beamer waited until she was reasonably sure that Sarah was awake, then called her. Sarah complained about the early phone call. "It's nine-thirty, for Pete's sake," said Beamer. "I've already sold buckets of bait."

"What do you want?"

"Any chance you'll run into Josh today?" Josh and Sarah were neighbors.

"Maybe. He usually goes with my brother to the gym to play basketball."

"Well, do me a favor and tell him that I'm still free and suddenly interested."

Simpson's was packed with its usual crowd. Beamer studied her barely touched slice of pie, then offered it to Josh, who ate it. They picked up their checks and coats and walked to the register. Beamer was behind Josh and felt dwarfed by his linebacker's bulk; he was the only date who had ever made her feel so small.

They paid, then Josh said, "Just a minute" and pushed through the crowd toward the restroom. Beamer leaned against the wall and waited, exchanging greetings with anyone she knew who passed by or yelled from afar. A classmate pulled her knit cap down over her face. Beamer had a few nasty thoughts about boys who weren't as funny as they thought, then lifted the cap. She was face to face with Andy.

He smiled. "I guess that means he loves you," he said.

"Rodents don't have feelings," she joked.

A girl appeared next to Andy. "Oh, hi, Beamer. Uh, Andy, I guess I'll go and warm up the car."

"I'll be right with you, Jacqueline."

Beamer watched the girl leave. She knew her only slightly, but wasn't surprised to see her with Andy. Jacqueline Snow was also an aspiring artist, and she was the daughter of Evelyn Snow, a painter of such renown that she was no longer ever labeled "Indian artist."

"Don't let me keep you, Andy."

"You won't. You're here with Josh, right? I'm surprised."

"Don't be. I'm not surprised to see you with Jacqueline. You two make a nice couple."

"May I call you tomorrow?"

"Please go, Andy," Beamer whispered.

"Beamo, let me tell you something. Sort of a warning."

"Jacqueline's waiting for you."

"There are two kinds of guys in the world. That's it — two. The guys who can't wait to get in the locker room and talk about what they do with their girlfriends, sexually speaking, and the guys who don't. I don't."

"And Josh?"

"I don't." Andy turned and left.

Josh returned, took her arm, and guided her out of the restaurant. "Did you and the sensitive artist have a nice talk?" he asked.

"Not especially."

While they paused to put on gloves, Beamer looked down the street. Snow was falling heavily. She saw a lone figure jogging along and for a moment thought it was Andy. She quickened and flushed. The man's face was illuminated under a street lamp as he reached a waiting car, and Beamer relaxed as the stranger drove away.

"Hey, are you still here?" Josh said.

Beamer looked at him. "I'm sorry, Josh. I guess I've been pretty lousy company tonight."

"That's true, but it doesn't matter." He stroked her neck above the collar of her unzipped jacket. "I figured all along it would get better later."

Beamer gently pushed his hand away. "Not a chance, Josh. Not a chance. Would you mind taking me home now?"

179

Daryl and Sandra's car was parked among others in the store's lot. For once Beamer was glad to see the cars still there. She pre-empted Josh's inevitable request for a kiss or a lingering goodnight.

"Josh, it looks like trouble again with family friends. It might be better if you didn't come in. Thanks for everything; I needed to get out."

She was out of the car and walking toward the door before he had done much more than mumble, "Sure, Beamer."

She entered through the back door. Children's voices came from the store. The grown-ups were upstairs. She put away her coat and gloves, then sat on the sofa to remove her boots. She sat still for several minutes, warming her toes in her hands and thinking about the evening. *Poor Josh. It was a bit cruel to go out and get his hopes up. Well, I will not feel too guilty. He'll find a party to go to and have a better time without me.*

She leaned back, resting against the coats piled on the sofa. She smiled slightly, remembering the number of times she and Andy had ended their evenings right here, avoiding the Woodies, talking and otherwise prolonging their goodnights. Then Beamer exhaled sharply and rose abruptly. *I'm glad I did it; let Jacqueline enjoy his company.* She pushed open the door to the hall and climbed the stairs.

The Woodies were in the kitchen, gathered around the table listening to Sandra. Beamer paused just outside the kitchen. Sandra was telling about the protest and the bomb.

180

Daryl was staring at his wife, and Beamer's father had a hand on his shoulder. Beamer listened to Sandra but watched the two men. They had been college roommates for two years and teammates on a notoriously bad football team. Now they were sitting with their friends and wives, listening to a story of manslaughter.

Candles burned on the table, the only light in the kitchen. The soft, flickering light played tricks: gray hairs were hidden, wrinkles smoothed. Beamer saw a room full of young dreamers.

Sandra finished. For a moment no one broke the silence. Then there was a bustle of action because no one could speak: Jenny stepped behind Sandra and gently massaged her shoulders; Peter collected tea mugs and carried them to the sink; Daniel stowed uneaten food in the refrigerator; Sue turned on a light; Maud blew out the candles, one by one.

Beamer went to her room. She watched through the window as the Woodies left — in families, in pairs, alone. Her parents escorted Daryl and Sandra, the last to go, and waited without their coats in the falling snow as their friends drove away. When the car had disappeared, they turned to each other and embraced, then walked hand in hand to the store.

Beamer returned to the kitchen and began tidying up, emptying cold tea into the sink and loading the dishwasher. She heard her mother enter and waited for her to speak.

"Bea, darling, I didn't hear you come in."

"I peeked in earlier. Where's Dad?"

"He went to the Wyatts' to get Johnny." Mrs. Flynn sat at the table. Beamer joined her.

"It looked like a pretty quiet group here tonight."

"Sandra and Daryl were here."

"I saw."

"She's decided to plead guilty. She'll be telling her lawyer on Monday."

"Why? I would have thought it would suit her purpose to have a public trial. It would give her a chance to publicize her cause."

"Right now she's more concerned about her family. She's convinced she'll be found guilty anyway, and she's decided she just wants to get on with it."

"What's next?"

"She'll plead, she'll be sentenced, she'll go to prison. Evidently the minimum sentence for manslaughter is four years, and even with parole she can expect to serve almost three. Three years in prison. Minimum."

Beamer had a memory flash — a fleeting, vivid picture of the young Sandra leading the children in the commune preschool in dance and games, her caftan swirling about her in waves of brilliant color. Three years in prison.

"Faith into action," she said.

"Yes," said Mrs. Flynn. "Well, this time it went wrong."

"Went wrong? Mom, a guy is dead. Dead!"

"Yes, dead. That's the horror of it, of course. That, and Sandra's going to prison." Mrs. Flynn settled back in the chair and rubbed her temples with her fingertips. "I don't think it was an easy decision for her to make, to cooperate with the authorities."

"So she and Daryl came here for the Woodies' vote of approval, right? You took a vote, guilty or not guilty. Cooperate or defy."

Mrs. Flynn's gaze was steady and strong. "They came to see their friends. They are going through a hell that can only get worse, and they wanted to be with friends."

Beamer couldn't meet her mother's eyes. She looked at the table, picked up a matchbook, and relit a candle. Her fingers traced the waxy bumps on its surface. Then she looked at her mother.

Mrs. Flynn was waiting. "Bea, I spent twelve years trying to carve out a new, different way of life. I failed. Now I am happy just to have a business that is part of the community and a home that's open to friends."

"So open that your own daughter feels crowded out."

"I'm sorry if I have failed to see that."

"Sometimes, Mom, it seems so ridiculous — after all these years the whole crowd is still sitting around, arguing over this, agreeing on that, taking votes on any little problem in somebody's life."

"We don't take votes; we listen." Mrs. Flynn's voice was sharp. "Beamer . . ." She paused, then lifted and cupped her hands, as if trying to shape the words, mold the clarity of what she was feeling. Her hands dropped and lay still in her lap. "Bea, I'm sorry you are hurting. But I am not sorry to have given you a life filled with people who love you."

"Fewer of them would have been okay, Mom."

Mrs. Flynn was smiling now. She rose, stretched, and yawned. "Maybe I agree with that, but then, how to pick and choose?"

"Vote."

Her mother's exasperation rekindled. "Oh, Bea, in a short enough time you will be my age, and Lord knows what you will have gone through by then, but if you are very lucky you will still have the friends who helped you survive." She reached and smoothed back the hair on her daughter's temples. "And if you are very, very lucky you will have a daughter who questions it all."

The candle sputtered and was extinguished in its own pool of wax.

Mrs. Flynn turned and moved toward the doorway. "I'm tired, Beamo. Goodnight."

Beamer held one hand tightly with the other. She had to say something, had to let her mother know that she had heard.

"Mom."

"Yes?"

"Don't think I hate all of you."

"None of us does."

"And it's not as if I totally hate my life, the way it's been."

"Good."

"But now I want it to be *my* life. Mine. I'm tired of being the group project."

"Beamer, you are not, and never have been, anybody's project. You are our daughter, Bob and Carolyn's child."

"You've had input."

Her mother smiled again. "That's true enough. And plenty of it."

The shadows and light were playing tricks again. Beamer looked at her mother and saw a tall, slender young woman, tired and just a bit unsure. Mrs. Flynn pulled down the cuffs of her sweater and then crossed her arms.

That sweater. Andy had — Beamer buried the thought.

"Yes?" her mother prompted.

"Yes what?"

"You're thinking something."

"It's nothing much. Just that once Andy told me he thought you were the prettiest woman he had ever seen. You were wearing that sweater the night he said it."

"He said that? Oh, I always did like Andy."

"You always did like flattery."

"No, dear. It's your father who loves flattery; I'm more detached." She considered saying more. Finally her curiosity subdued her caution. "Bea, don't you miss Andy?"

"No."

Mrs. Flynn arched her eyebrows. "I'm your mother, Beamo. You can't get a lie past me."

"Maybe I miss his company."

"I'll accept that. Perhaps —"

"Mom, we've talked enough tonight, okay?"

"Just one more bit of advice?"

"If you must."

"I just hope you didn't break off with him when it was really the Woodies you wanted to chase away."

Just what Andy had said. Beamer didn't answer.

Mrs. Flynn yawned. "Don't tell our friends, Beamo, but I'll confess that sometimes your father and I are very happy to chase them away. Tonight I was glad to see them go."

"The two of you looked pretty cute outside, hugging in the snow."

"Shame on you for watching."

"I often do. I see a lot."

Mrs. Flynn nodded almost imperceptibly. "I'm sure you do." She flexed her shoulders to chase away the end-of-day stiffness, and shoved her hands into her sweater pockets. She pulled out a handful of paper scraps. "Charade commands."

"Sandra's going off to prison and you played the same old games?"

"We stopped when they arrived. Oh, don't be so disapproving. Beamer, as you muddle through life you'll discover the things you can't change and the things you can't escape. Sometimes the best you can do," she said, sprinkling the paper scraps over the table, "is to have a little fun. Goodnight, Bea."

"Goodnight, Mom."

CHAPTER
· 19 ·

Martin returned the night the Woodies were all at the store celebrating Mr. Flynn's birthday. Beamer had tried her civil best to enjoy the occasion and be pleasant to everyone. She had led the younger children in building snow statues; she had helped her mother bake and decorate the cake; she had personally supervised the outdoor grilling of the tofu-and-crushed-walnut burgers, enduring the cold wind and deep snow so that her father could have his favorite food on his birthday. She had even been cajoled into joining his team for charades and was just beginning her turn when Martin arrived.

Everyone flocked around the newcomer, who greeted them all cheerfully. The group then broke up for refreshments. Martin took Beamer aside and hugged her warmly. He stepped back, laughing. "Don't panic."

"I wasn't."

"Stiff as a board. I was just saying hello."

Maud passed them, and Martin teased her about

her newly permed and gray-free hair. Maud feigned insult and turned away.

"I've been dying to say something about her hair all week," said Beamer. "I didn't dare."

"Take a chance, girl," said Martin.

The Woodies reassembled around the stove and called loudly to Beamer to resume playing charades.

"It's your turn? What have you got?" Martin asked. Beamer showed him the slip: "The Collected Poems of Emily Dickinson." "Oh, I can figure out how to do that one," he said. "Let me take it for you." Beamer nodded. She stood to the side, laughing along with the others as Martin pantomimed the title. As he performed, Beamer suddenly, clearly, remembered her mother's words on the night they talked in the kitchen. "Sometimes the best you can do," she repeated silently, "is to have a little fun."

Martin finished to a round of applause. He bowed ostentatiously, then said he was leaving. At the door he signaled to Beamer. "May I have my keys? I'm beat — I want to go home."

She retrieved the keys from a hook behind the store counter and handed them to him.

"Thanks."

"Are you sure you can't stay any longer?"

"I don't think I can cope with this craziness anymore."

"Neither can I. It's been going on since noon. You wouldn't be interested in driving back to Chicago and taking me for company, would you?"

"Car wouldn't make it. I've got something for

you, though," he said. "Can you stand the cold for a minute?"

It had been snowing all evening, and Beamer wiped Martin's windshield clear with her hand while he rummaged in a duffel bag on the back seat. "Here we go," he said. "I knew they were here somewhere." First he handed her a limp wrapped package. "Nothing special, okay? Just a late birthday present." Then he gave her a large brown envelope. "I want you to read this. It's a story I wrote that was just accepted for publication by the university literary magazine."

"Martin, that's great. You've never told me you write fiction."

"Just one of my many secrets, Merry. I hope you like it."

"I'm sure I will."

"And if you don't, well, never mind. You'll understand after you read it."

"Understand what?"

He kissed her softly on the cheek. "See you soon."

She opened the package in her room. It was a dark blue hooded sweatshirt from Northwestern University, Martin's school.

She prepared for bed before reading the story. Then she propped pillows, lit a candle, turned on her reading lamp, and crawled under the comforter. She opened the envelope and pulled out the sheaf of papers. "Everybody's Daughter," she read. "Everybody's Daughter"?

She read the story through twice, then laid the papers down on her chest. She understood Martin's

189

concern. The story was about her — about her family, their life, their friends, but mostly about her.

"Why did you do this?" she whispered. She scanned the story again, and her eyes fell on a passsage that had caught her interest the first time. She read it aloud:

The object of everybody's passion, everybody's hope, everybody's love, she had built a wall, as if that alone could protect her from being smothered. Cold and distant, she stayed hidden behind the wall. He wondered how long she could remain alone, resisting the hand that waited to guide her to the place where it would be safe to love.

Beamer put the story on the floor, lay back, and stared at a shadowy corner of the room. What had he been thinking when he wrote that? Sarah had said he was just waiting for a signal. Was he? Were those few casual kisses his signal? And what about his girl-friend? She recalled his silly pantomime of the book title. And the good feeling she'd had when he'd arrived unexpectedly. Take a chance, he'd said. Beamer smiled. Maybe Sarah was right. Maybe it was time to ride out of town on the back of someone's motorcycle. Martin had said he had one.

She had to talk to him. She had to make him talk. "No jokes. No quick kisses and no glib jokes," she said aloud.

The next day it was so cold that the few travelers and fishermen who stopped by the store didn't even pretend to like winter weather. They paid for their purchases silently, sullenly, as if they had been physically assaulted by the cold and were now entirely alone in their misery.

Beamer left the store, ignoring her parents' appeals not to go out. Her parents, she had long ago discovered, disapproved of much but forbade little. They trusted her judgment.

The bright sun and clear sky belied the frigidity. By the time she reached the north shore clearing, her lungs ached and her fingers were numb. She warmed her hands between her thighs for a moment, then skied on. When she reached Martin's cabin her eyelashes were iced over and heavy. Leaving her skis and poles in the snow, she pounded on the door and entered. Martin rose from the sofa — he had been reading — and led Beamer to the fire. He took her mittens and offered her a tissue.

"Why in the world did you come out today?" he asked.

"To see you, obviously. It wasn't that bad. I kept moving."

Martin took Beamer's hat and wiped ice crystals from her brow. Then he warmed her cheeks with the backs of his hands. She covered his hands with her own, squeezed them, and sighed.

Martin stepped back. He hadn't needed a word to understand, and now he was unhappy. "Oh, God, Merry," he said. "Oh, please, not that. When you broke up with Andy, I started worrying that this would happen. Do you think I'm an idiot? I thought

191

you would understand." He turned and called, "Daniel, Merry is here."

Daniel entered from the bathroom. He had been thawing frozen pipes — an innocent task; he was a plumber — but to Beamer, who glowered at her old friend, he might as well have been a rapist stalking a victim.

Beamer refused the offer of a ride and left when her mittens were dry. Her rhythm was gone, she could find no words to chant or tune to hum, and the skiing was difficult. She fell twice, and the frozen crust scraped her bared wrists. She stopped at the clearing to rest and to swear at Martin and to swear at herself for being so stupid. Wondering what had happened, she resisted the desire to throw herself into the lake — it was frozen, anyway — and did not jab with her ski pole at a fallen, frozen chickadee. A strong wind had risen and brought in clouds. Beamer lowered her head and skied home, a long, slow trip into a cold and biting wind.

The wind removed the cold but brought in a cycle of four blizzards, each lasting two days. After the second storm the schools were closed and store deliveries stopped. No one bought bait. Beamer's parents and brother were caught by the fourth storm in Grand River. "We won't try to get home until tomorrow," her father said on the phone. "Peter and Sue are near if you need them."

Jessie called twice, the first time to complain of her new boyfriend's inattention.

192

"It's your own fault, Jessie," said Beamer. "You grovel like he's Prince Charming, and he thinks he can get away with murder."

Jessie hung up but called back immediately. "This weather makes us all crazy and grumpy, so I forgive you. Besides, I forgot to tell you I saw Andy in town on Saturday."

"Was he with Jacqueline?"

"No. His sisters. He asked about you."

"What did you say?"

"I said you'd made a move on Martin and it blew up in your face and now you wanted to get back together."

"Jessie!"

"Just kidding. I told him you missed him."

"I don't."

"You do."

"You're wrong."

"No, I'm not. Now stop it. He gave me a message for you. Do you want it?"

"Yes."

"He said, 'Tell her I won't cross any lines. Tell her the thermostat is fixed and running steady.' He said you'd understand. I know I don't."

Beamer smiled. "I do."

"So, Bea?"

"Jessie, you know I like Andy. I like him a lot. But you also know how I feel about the relationship."

"Relationship? Oh, Bea, get real. Most of us just want boyfriends; you want a relationship."

Beamer didn't answer.

"Are you there? Andy may have his flaws, Beamo, but next to a sleazeball like Martin, who spends weeks teasing you with kisses and warm chats by the fire and then just uses your life to get published, he looks pretty good. Martin used you. He used you, he used you. He comes up here for a few months and thinks he'll mend his broken heart by playing with every female who gives him a second look. And then the first chance he gets, he goes running back to his girlfriend. Which is exactly what you should do."

"Go back to my girlfriend?"

"You know what I mean. Face it — Martin was fun, but he was just playing with you."

"Oh, Jessie, I don't know what I want."

"You want what everyone our age wants — a magician. A little hocus-pocus and *poof,* your life is changed."

"How did you get so wise?"

"I didn't. Andy said that."

"He said that about me?"

"Right on target, isn't it? Kind of scary, if you ask me. So will you give it another chance? I'll call him for you, and then he can make the move."

"Jessie, you have no idea what kind of year it has been, with Daniel out of the hospital and hanging around and Sandra killing a guy. And then all the normal stuff my parents bring home. Just this huge crush of people, and on top of it, Andy wants to get closer."

"With all that crazy stuff going on, I'd think you would like a shoulder to rest on."

"You do love to meddle, don't you?"

"Then I can call him?"

"No."

"Oh, you are an idiot."

"I'll call him myself. Jessie . . ."

"Spit it out, Beamo."

Beamer closed her eyes and saw what she had first seen — a strange, smiling boy lying on the ground with a broken leg. "I think I've missed him."

"Tell *him*, not me. When will you call?"

"Maybe not today."

"But you'll call?"

"I'll call."

They chatted longer, then hung up. Beamer made a cake, and while it baked she cleaned her room. She thumbed through a textbook and read exercise advice in a magazine. She ate hot, crumbling cake and drank a glass of cold milk. She thought she liked being alone, but realized she didn't want it to go on forever.

The phone rang. It was Martin. Beamer caught her breath, then answered casually. She was cool; she was in control.

"Is anyone there?" Martin asked.

"I don't count?"

"Of course you do. But I need help. Daniel has crushed his foot. His car got stuck in a drift, and we were pushing it out. He slipped and the damn thing rolled back over his foot and smashed it against a

195

rock. He's really hurting, Merry. And my car battery is dead, so I can't drive him out. He's waiting in his car."

Beamer quickly calculated the risks and options and said, "Try to get him back to your place. I'll call the highway patrol. With luck they can get here, and meanwhile I'll come for Daniel on the snowmobile. There's no one else."

Rescuing someone in a blizzard was a fool's mission, but Beamer felt up to the task. The family seldom used the snowmobile, but it would be ready, gassed and greased; her parents kept things in order, she could rely on that.

The engine's roar was deafening, even through the helmet. Beamer knew many people who rode snowmobiles for pleasure, but she had never understood why. She sped over the trail, jolting and lunging over the dips and rises, finding her way by chance and memory through the tumult of wind and snow. When she got to the cabin, Martin was waiting outside.

"He's still in the car," Martin said. "He wouldn't budge. I just got back from taking him some coffee. The car isn't too far, just beyond the second curve. I'll come with you."

"I can manage alone."

"Did you get the patrol?"

"I couldn't get through, so I called Sue. She's trying. How bad is it?"

"Hard to say — the foot is bleeding, or was when I left, but very slowly. I took his boot off to wrap a bandage around it. The coloring looks bad, what I could see. Look, the three of us could probably push the car out."

"Three of us?"

"Katie is here." He tilted his head toward the cabin. "That's why Daniel drove out. My car battery was dead, so I asked him to pick her up at the bus station."

"In this weather, Martin? Couldn't she have spent the night at Jenny's? Or Elizabeth's? Elizabeth certainly owes you a favor."

"I wanted to see her tonight. She's only got two days here. Daniel could have said no."

"You don't mind using people, do you?"

"I'll get Katie. Let's push him out."

"Don't bother. I can have him home by the time we'd dig the car out. And it would probably just slide back in another few feet. No, I'll take him." She walked a few steps, then turned. Martin was nearly hidden by the thick wall of falling, blowing snow.

"Martin, you could have told me you still had Katie on the line."

He walked closer, digging his hands into his pockets. "Well, I didn't. Not until I went home."

"I don't like embarrassing myself, Martin. And I don't like people playing with me."

"A few kisses, Merry. Don't take it all so seriously."

"And the invitation to spend the summer together? Or did you invite all the other women you've been hustling too? That would have been some summer party."

"I just thought you'd be happier if you got out of here."

"And the story, Martin? What was that you wrote? 'How long could she resist the hand . . .' "

"Fiction."

"Fiction? You used me for fiction? That doesn't feel so good, Martin."

"I used Andy too. Remember what you told me he said when you two broke up? Those are his thoughts. I stole them." He shifted weight. "Merry, wise up. If there's any guy patiently holding out his hand for you, it's Andy. Not me. Andy."

"Then why did you do it, Martin? Why did you have to come on like you were just waiting for something, and then turn it into a story?"

"You're really mad, aren't you? Hey, remember the day we met? I promised to stifle a desire to snoop. But I didn't promise not to watch."

"That day I skied to your cabin — what was that about being an idiot?"

"That was harsh. Sorry."

"Yes, it was. What did you mean?"

Martin waited, then spoke slowly. "Merry, you are as beautiful a girl as I have seen in a long time. And terrific company. But I'm no fool." He stepped closer.

Beamer crossed her arms and shifted her weight. Martin stopped.

"The guy who gets you gets the Woodies. I've had fun with them this winter, but that's all I want. When next term begins at school, I'm gone, and I don't want to come back for every damn holiday, or birthday, or baby, or bombing. Andy can take it on; I won't."

A dark figure appeared in the cabin window. Martin saw it, then again moved closer to Beamer. "Besides, Katie means too much for me to risk losing her for some entanglement with a high school girl."

High school girl. The statement of fact was like a slap.

"Well, if she means so much to you, I hope you burned your phone list before she arrived. It might upset her to know how you were mending your broken heart."

"I put it away. She won't get upset."

"Put it away! You mean it comes back out as soon as she goes? What about entanglements?"

"Doesn't apply to those girls."

Beamer shook her head. "Martin, don't the people in your life have any meaning for you?"

Martin tucked his hands under his arms. "I'm sorry for what went wrong. Does it have to change everything?" He reached tentatively to touch Beamer, then stuffed his hand into his jeans pocket. "Please, Merry, I don't want to lose this friendship." He smiled broadly and his voice lightened. "You're the best skiing buddy I've ever had."

Beamer looked again at Katie's silhouette, then at Martin. "Skiing buddy?" She shook her head. "I don't think that would be fair to Andy. It's time I start thinking about that. I'm going to get Daniel."

Daniel had the car engine off and the radio on. Beamer slid into the driver's seat. "Well, Moonbeam, hello," he said.

"This is lousy weather for delivering girlfriends, Daniel."

"You sound just like your mother when you lecture, Beamo."

"How's the foot?"

"Hurts." He closed his eyes. "It hurts quite a lot." She looked at his calm, unshaven profile, a face so familiar she could conjure its details with her eyes closed.

"I'll take you home, Daniel."

"Will you, Moonbeam? I'm only an old hippie, hardly deserving of the help."

She punched him lightly on the arm. "Stuff the sarcasm, old man. You're in pain, remember? Let's drag you home now."

He sat behind her on the snowmobile with his arms around her waist. She retraced her path around the lake, and anticipating the rough trail this time, she slowed down. Still, with every jolt Daniel moaned, a low vibration against her back. At the clearing she stopped and stepped off. She knelt and checked the bandage on his foot, rewrapping it and tucking in the trailing, bloody ends. She surveyed the path ahead and the empty expanse of frozen lake. The blizzard was letting up, and Beamer could see the light of the patrol car parked by the bait shop, the rotating red beam cutting a swath through the snow. She got back on the snowmobile and wrapped Daniel's arms around her.

"Moonbeam," Daniel shouted above the engine's drone, "I saw you being born. I was there."

200

"No, you weren't, Daniel. You were asleep in the kitchen."

"Well, I've seen the pictures. That counts."

She squeezed his hand, and they resumed their ride home against a lighter snowfall and weaker wind. This storm was over.